The Amish Farmer Who Hated L.A.

This collection of short stories warms the heart and provides insight into how God is at work through people today. The stories take biblical topics and situate them in contemporary cultural settings and so help open our eyes to their meaning for today. Tim Reddish takes on a number of interesting topics and handles them with grace.

> Dr. John Sanders, professor of religious studies
> Hendrix College; author of *The God Who Risks*

In this book, the delights of imagination meet timeless stories of Scripture. The outcome is the retelling of deep truths about both the human condition and God's remarkable grace. Tim Reddish has given us a whimsical and thought-provoking read that is also pure pleasure.

> Rev. Dr. Judy Paulsen, professor of evangelism
> Wycliffe College, Toronto

Tim Reddish writes to address difficult questions from interesting angles. His work feels fresh, contemporary, challenging and thought-provoking—without departing from orthodox faith. This book helps us to reflect on our lives, the better to serve the One who gave us life.

> Ven. Nick Barker, archdeacon of Auckland
> priest-in-charge of Holy Trinity, Darlington, UK

In reading each of Tim's stories, I had an *"Aha!"* moment when I realized which familiar Bible story he was depicting, only to discover an unexpected twist around the next corner. These stories are full of gentle humor and great insight that will keep the reader thinking for days after reading them.

> Rev. Dr. Stuart Macdonald, professor of church and society,
> Knox College, Toronto

and 8 other modern-day allegories

Tim Reddish

The Amish Farmer Who Hated L.A.
Copyright ©2015 by Tim Reddish

Published by
Deep River Books
Sisters, Oregon
www.deepriverbooks.com

All rights reserved. No part of this book may be reproduced or transmitted in any form or by any means, electronic or mechanical, including photocopying and recording, or by any information storage and retrieval system, without permission in writing from the publisher.

Although based on real events as recorded in The Holy Bible, this is a work of fiction. Any resemblance to persons living or dead is purely coincidental.

ISBN: 9781940269566
Library of Congress: 2015906644

Printed in the USA

Cover design by Joe Bailen

In Memory of:

Anne, my wife
Dennis, my dad
Ruth, my sister

To Philip, Greer, and Arthur
Adam, Andrew, Jonathan, and Julia

Contents

	Preface 11
	Acknowledgments......................... 13
One	The Dawn 15
Two	The Amish Farmer Who Hated L.A. 27
Three	The God-Man Project..................... 39
Four	The First Day 51
Five	The Sermon 63
Six	The Journey 73
Seven	The Nightmare........................... 83
Eight	The Audience............................ 91
Nine	The Apocalypse 103
	For Further Thought..................... 115
	Endnotes................................ 127

PREFACE

THESE SHORT ALLEGORICAL or Midrash-like stories are based on biblical incidents or themes, yet retold in fresh ways, sometimes with subtle wit and humor, or with a surprising twist.[1] As you read, see how long it takes you to guess the original biblical story on which it is based. Cultural distance and over-familiarity often cause the biblical narratives to fail to shock or challenge us and hence prevent their influence and power to transform our lives. Such inadvertent taming of the text is something that the Gospel writers would decry. As the great storyteller C. S. Lewis reminds us, Aslan, the lion of Narnia, is not tame—but he is good! Whether we are Christians or not, our preconceived ideas about the Bible provide a lens through which we read and understand its contents. That lens—or worldview—is shaped by many factors, including our religious tradition, family systems, and education, which are influenced by the Enlightenment. We should, however, always be self-critical of our assumptions—ask any scientist. If you find yourself shocked, it may be your "lens" being challenged, rather than the Bible itself.

It is my hope that you find these stories interesting and engaging, and that they stimulate further reflection and discussion. To help kindle that process, at the back of the book there is a "For Further Thought" section containing suggested Bible readings and discussion questions. Naturally, some might react to the theological bias that I deliberately—and at times, provocatively—inject into some of the tales. Others will find these views resonating with their own. Remember, this is storytelling, not a nuanced academic work. While these stories are for enjoyment, they are also meant to relate serious points. Humor catches us off guard, allowing a story's message to penetrate our hearts. One way or another, my hope is that you will let them speak to you, and in so doing, begin a process that allows the Spirit to revitalize your understanding of God.

Tim Reddish

Acknowledgments

I WOULD LIKE TO BEGIN by acknowledging Andrew and Mary Templer. Mary, now retired, was the founding minister of University Community Church (UCC) in Windsor. She and Andrew have closely followed all aspects of my journey over the last twelve years since coming to Canada. Thank you for encouraging and supporting me in my transition from physics to theology and for urging me to pursue writing as part of my future. I would also like to thank Frank and Ruth Homme who patiently and excitedly heard and read the first drafts of these stories. I recall your chuckles and delight with great fondness, even though you thought I was perhaps being too provocative at times!

In addition to my parents and family, there have been many people who have helped shape my life over the years; the members of the Thursday Night Group and all at UCC in Windsor; Russ and Ann Rusby and the home group in Whitley Bay; St. James and Emmanuel, Didsbury; my life-long friend Peter Hammond now in Perth, Australia. For all the experiences we have shared, happy and sad, thank you.

More recently, I have been a student at Knox College, Toronto. I express my thanks to my professors and fellow seminary students, especially Mandy, Neil, Anita, Stephen, and Seaton. We have learned so much together, having our minds and faith stretched in new ways. Thank you for all you have taught me.

As I look to my bookshelves, I acknowledge the authors who have influenced my theology over the decades. Authors such as C. S. Lewis, John Stott, Michael Green, Lesslie Newbigin,

John Polkinghorne, Clark Pinnock, Brian McLaren, and N. T. Wright. And, of course, Adrian Plass, who taught me to laugh at myself and the Church. Thank you for your wisdom and insights.

To the whole team at Deep River Books, especially my editor, Caryn Rivadeneira, I say a big "thank you" for making this book the best it can be. I also acknowledge the Writer's Edge for publicizing this work, so enabling it to be noticed by potential publishers.

And finally, and—of course—by no means least, I thank my wife, Mary. Thank you for sharing this exciting new journey into directions we, as yet, do not know. Thank you for your patience in reading the early manuscript, and making many excellent suggestions to improve the text. I love you.

Chapter One

THE DAWN

THE WARM RAYS of the rising sun shone on to the entrance of the large south-facing cave. Some of the cave dwellers were already busy starting the daily campfire with dried grass and twigs. The cave itself was ideally situated on a small outcrop of boulders, with a good view of the forest below and the lazy crystal clear river that flowed towards the nearby lake. From this vantage point they could see a long way to the mountains beyond and hear distant sounds travelling over the valley. The dawn chorus from kingfishers, weavers, and other colorful birds was heard by the cave dwellers. But, alas, they did not perceive it as the enchanting melody it was.

Their life was simple and, to a great extent, carefree, since there were no significant predators—at least not where they lived. The cave dwellers were all naked and no one seemed to care. There was a familiar routine, though it did not seem monotonous. The children collected the kindling and wood from the forest. The women daily brought fresh water from the river within hollowed-out dried gourds. During the day some of the families went down to the river to catch tilapia, which were plentiful. Other women and children picked berries, plums, tamarinds, and wild apricots. The older men showed the younger boys how to find special stones for axes, spears, and arrowheads. Everyone had a role in making coarse ropes and finer twine from vines, bulrush reeds, and other plant fibers. These were then used to make snares and nets, as well as fastenings for their stone tools.

In this manner, parents passed on their crafts and skills to their children, who were always eager to participate in what often appeared to be an enjoyable game. The parents took delight, knowing that in turn their children would pass on the same knowledge to their own offspring.

Occasionally small groups of travellers would pass through their encampment. They would stay awhile, swap stories and information. Some of the nomads would settle with the cave dwellers. In turn, some of the younger families would move on with the wayfarers. In this way communities gradually intermingled. It had been this way for generations. No one could remember anything else.

However, it was clear to these cave dwellers that one individual was quite different from the rest of the community. We will call him Terrene, although he did not yet know that was his name. He was now a young man, but even as a youth he had been more difficult than the others, continually asking *Why?*

More and more frequently, Terrene refused to follow the routine established by the community's elders and challenged their authority. It was not that he was mischievous or malicious; he was just unusual. For instance, he would create new tools that did a better job than the established ones. Occasionally they were appreciated, but most times they were not. The elders would shake their heads in dismay at Terrene and sometimes showed their displeasure by breaking the tools that he had made. Terrene would vocalize his frustration, and then disappear on his own to cool off for a while. Nobody seemed to understand him.

One particular morning as Terrene walked out of the cave to the rising sun, he saw flares of red, purple, and yellow splashed across the dawn sky reflecting from the clouds and the river. He also noticed the gentle rustle of the wind in the trees and heard the birds sing against the background sound of the babbling water. Terrene stood still. After a while, he thought, *This is so beautiful*. Somehow he had never seen his surroundings in this way before. Terrene glanced around at his clan to see whether they also comprehended what he saw. As he looked into their eyes, he realized they were oblivious. Terrene was the only person who recognized this sight as actually being magnificent or heard the bird song as music.

This made Terrene's apparent waywardness even more difficult for the other cave dwellers to tolerate. It did not take long for his relatives to show their increasing dislike of him. Inspired by his new perception of the world around him, Terrene used vivid mineral paints to draw pictures on the cave walls of the sun, moon, and familiar animals. The others watched in bewilderment and failed to appreciate his artwork. Certain key elders even defaced some of his drawings. Although no one there could articulate the situation in these terms, the others in this small community felt threatened by Terrene's behavior. Since he wouldn't submit to the elders, Terrene could not be relied upon to pass on their collective knowledge to the next generation. Nobody wanted to associate with him. They realized instinctively that for the sake of their long-term survival, Terrene must go. The elders indicated in words and by gestures that Terrene was no longer welcome and must leave their community. He went back into the cave, collected his few tools and deer hide, and then walked to the edge of the clearing around which they all had lived together. He turned for one final look and saw young children playing; they were unaware of this unfolding drama. Terrene looked at the adults who were staring at him, as if daring him to try and stay. Drooping his shoulders, Terrene waved to show he posed no threat and held no malice. He then walked forward into the forest and did not look back again.

Terrene walked for many weeks; he forded waterways, explored new valleys—and avoided other cave-dwelling communities. After a while he came across a lone tree trunk that had fallen across a swift flowing river. He walked across the large log—careful to maintain his balance—and went into the waiting woods with his few belongings. Over the next few weeks, Terrene explored this new region. He discovered it was a huge island surrounded by wide rivers. Indeed the island was so large that he could not measure its dimensions. It contained new types of plants and trees, as well as the familiar ones. There were several spectacular waterfalls and gurgling springs; a scenic haven amid what was already a relatively easy land for people to thrive. He decided that in this pleasing region he would make his new home, and so he began to look for another suitable cave.

In a place not too far from Terrene's new home, much nearer than one would think—just in the next dimension—a Watcher came to the Maker. She said, "Lord, I have observed something that you may be interested in seeing for yourself. Remember how you asked all Watchers to keep a keen eye among the forest campsites for unusual behavior? Well, I have identified something that merits closer attention." The Watcher explained to the Maker how it was her responsibility to overlook this particular cave-dwelling community. She recognized that Terrene's actions resulted in him being forced to leave. What struck the Watcher as odd was that Terrene had departed alone. People always travelled in families or small groups, she explained, and a lone wanderer was unique in her experience.

"I wanted to bring this to your attention, Lord," concluded the Watcher, "as something is happening here that is most definitely out of the ordinary."

The Maker was excited to hear of this development and praised the Watcher for her vigilance. After he had reviewed all the information, he called a special and urgent meeting of his highest Council and invited the Watcher to attend.

The Maker had not called an urgent meeting of the Grand Council for a long time. Attendants looked at each other, whispering to their nearest neighbors, in the hope of having a hint of what was on the agenda. Their unanswered speculations were silenced as the Maker himself entered the chamber wearing the most spectacular robes imaginable. Everyone stood until he was seated at the head of the large oval table. The Maker then introduced the Watcher to the members of the Grand Council and invited her to tell Terrene's story. Once the Watcher had finished her detailed report, there was a spontaneous round of loud applause. The assembled dignitaries wanted to ask the Watcher questions, which the Maker permitted for a short time. Joy and anticipation spread throughout the room, but no one expected to hear what was said next.

When the Maker spoke, everyone listened.

"I have waited a long time for this moment," the Maker said. "A very long time indeed, and I have decided to go and visit Terrene myself."

Such a hush fell within the Council that one could hear the sharp intakes of breath from one or two delegates. The Council members looked at each other and eventually one of them asked, "If you visit Terrene will he not be terrified by your magnificent presence?"

"Not if I temporarily become embodied in a human-like form," the Maker replied.

This drew more gasps from around the room and several quick responses:

"This is totally unprecedented and highly dangerous."

"Are you sure this course of action is wise?"

"Why not simply send a Messenger?"

"But what about the Adversary?"

The Maker raised his hand for silence and, maintaining full composure, addressed them all.

"Terrene has demonstrated clear signs of a new level of consciousness and independence," the Maker said. "He is creative and curious, just as we wanted him to be. Right now he is totally and innocently absorbed in this fresh mode of discovery and fascinated by all that is around him. But soon he will realize that he is full of questions and has few answers. Moreover, with his maturing self-awareness, it will eventually dawn on him that he is, in fact, all alone—at which point he will experience anxiety and sorrow. This I want to avoid at all costs. As you all know, I never intended any created agent to be alone but to live in community. That is why all my creatures are in families. Even I am not alone. Terrene needs to have his questions answered and only I can give such an account. He must be told of his identity as my beloved son and be welcomed to our great family. Terrene also should know his role and responsibilities. Who else can tell him all this but his Maker?"

They all listened in thoughtful silence and pondered his words.

"Now," the Maker continued, "concerning the Adversary: he does not know or understand my ways and thinks I am self-centered and arrogant. He would imagine that if I condescended to such a visit at all, it would be in a fanfare of glory: a public, royal spectacle for all to witness. He will not expect such an incognito, low-key visit. And this gives us the advantage, at least for the moment. A lone wanderer, like Terrene, makes him a vulnerable prey for the Enemy's further meddling. The Adversary is no fool, and I expect him to turn up sooner or later."

After further discussion, which the Maker always welcomed, it was clear to the whole Council that the Maker loved Terrene as much as he loved them. There was no stopping the Maker in carrying out his daring plan.

One day Terrene heard the breaking of a twig behind him and turned his head instinctively towards the sound. To his surprise, he saw another person who looked like himself. The person was now sitting on rock, smiling, with a reassuring posture indicating no menace.

The Maker, initiating the conversation, said to Terrene, "I have come to help you and to show you many new and exciting things."

Terrene moved toward the Maker. "Who are you?" he asked gently.

"I am your Maker and the Creator of all you see on the land and in the sky. I know everything that can be known."

Terrene thought for few minutes and then asked, "Who am I?"

The Maker replied, "Your name is Terrene and you are my beloved son."

The Maker then instigated an intimate bear hug and both of them laughed out loud. All who watched in the next dimension celebrated this special moment in cosmic time with song and dance.

The Maker and Terrene met most evenings to talk. Terrene would come armed with questions and the Maker would answer them. As time went on, Terrene learned that the Maker was knowledgeable, wise, gentle, and kind.

The Maker had long known that Terrene would need a close companion with whom Terrene could share himself and all his newly found knowledge and experiences. It was not that Terrene was sad or lonely, but that Terrene had never met someone of his own kind who could appreciate the world in the same way he could. Late one afternoon, a young woman carrying her scanty belongings made her way delicately across the log bridge onto Terrene's island. Once hidden amongst the dense foliage, she felt safe from those who had chased her into exile. Having managed to outwit them several days ago in the forest, she expected they would soon lose interest in finding her and return to their communities.

After walking for a while, she stumbled across Terrene's clearing by his cave. Terrene saw her and beckoned her to come to the fire and share his food. Although she was tired and hungry, she wasn't sure whether or not to trust Terrene. But then she saw the Maker nearby. "Oh it's you again!" she exclaimed. "What are you doing here?"

"Zoë," said the Maker, "I have been waiting for you. Let me introduce you to Terrene." Now relaxed, Zoë came close to

Terrene, and they looked into each other's faces. They could both see that the other's eyes were alive with excitement and awareness.

The Maker then went away and left them.

As the sun was setting, Terrene and Zoë swapped their stories by the campfire. Birds, perched in the nearby trees, heard their laughter.

One evening the Maker came to visit them again. Looking directly at them, he said, "I want you both to know that I love each of you very deeply. My love is even stronger than the way you feel about each other—if you can possibly imagine that! I am committed to you and your future children's children forever and nothing will ever break my word."

The Maker paused for a moment to let his son and daughter absorb that declaration before continuing.

"Moreover," he said. "I have made you with special capabilities. To be creative, to explore, to make choices, to be responsible, and to experience loving relationships with your own kind and with me. All that you see around you is yours, and I want you to appreciate its goodness. I am entrusting you with the task of taking care of this land and making good and wise choices on my behalf. You can see all around you the results of decisions I have made. And you know me well enough by now to know the kind of choices that I would make. Your happiness will be complete if you keep listening to—and for—my voice."

It was not long after that conversation that Terrene began to think thoughts that had never entered his mind before.

Everything that he and Zoë did came easily to them, for nothing they did was perceived to be hard work. Terrene began to feel proud of his achievements and wanted to build bigger and better things simply because he could. He wanted to do things himself and didn't want to follow the wisdom and guidance the Maker had given. A voice in his head asked, "How can I *really* be sure he is the Maker? Can I trust him? Why does the Maker think he knows what is best for me? Isn't that attitude just like that of the elders? In escaping from their restrictions I became free. I don't want to follow. I want to lead."

Around the same time Zoë was having similar rebellious ideas of her own.

One evening the Maker came to visit them. Terrene and Zoë now had secrets that they wanted to keep from the Maker. They were more guarded in what they said to him, and he knew that there wasn't the same openness that there had been before. The Maker was sad to see this change in them, for it was not what he had wanted or expected to happen.

The Maker gently challenged them about their change in attitude and behavior. Having listened to their replies, he said to them both, "Terrene and Zoë, I knew such a day might come. But I had hoped such a day would never come. I have given you everything, including my total devotion. Your recent words and actions show that you are interested in yourselves and in creation but not in the life-giving Creator. Can you not see beyond the beauty of all that is around you and acknowledge the One who gave it to you? Can you not anticipate by now that there is much more to life than what you have yet experienced? Can you not recognize that your life will never be truly whole unless you include me within it?"

But Terrene and Zoë were no longer listening.

The Grand Council was again in session and the somber mood was in stark contrast to that of the previous meeting. Deep sorrow was evident in the face of the Maker and even the Comforter was sad.

"There is no disguising that we have experienced a major setback," said the Maker. "To say that Terrene and Zoë's illogical actions are heartbreaking and disappointing is a gross understatement. But that is the choice of my children, and I am honor-bound to respect the freedom I have given them."

"Perhaps you have given them too much freedom," one delegate muttered.

"This was always a high-risk undertaking," replied the Maker. "But I have no regrets. Right now they have rejected trust and relationship thinking that self-governance is to be valued above all. They will, however, eventually discover that it is the treasure and security of lasting mutual commitment that they will desire most. Ultimately, it is to be loved with no conditions that they will long for. This was, is, and will always be the essence of the gift of myself to them. Authentic love—since it can never be coerced—necessitates genuine liberty to give, receive, and—indeed—even reject it. The bond I desire to have with them is based on love, which is why it was necessary to make them truly free. That is simply the logic of love; there is no other way."

The Maker paused, and no one said anything.

He then continued, "The Adversary's subtlety has deceived them and right now he and his followers are celebrating a major victory. But fear not: this matter is not yet over. It has only just begun. My ultimate goals will never be thwarted. In the future it will be necessary to use a variety of other creative methods to communicate my boundless love to my sons and daughters. While this first plan has been foiled, I have many other plans and possibilities. I am never at a loss for ingenuity!"

He looked at all the dignitaries around the oval table and announced, "This meeting is closed."

The Maker then went quietly to his private chambers to grieve.

Chapter Two

THE AMISH FARMER WHO HATED L.A.

I AM A JOURNALIST. I've been one all my adult life. For many years I've lived out of a suitcase, traveling all around the world, reporting mainly on its hot spots: riots, terrorist attacks, wars, that kind of thing. I was good at it. My award-winning pieces enabled me to pick my newspaper, so I based myself in New York and worked for the *Times* for many years. Mike, my editor, gave me a lot of freedom and put his neck on the line for me many times, but I always managed a scoop with a different angle, like an original line from a boots-on-the-ground General or a whisper from a senior politician. Although I enjoyed the buzz of journalism, it was a rough life—too many cigarettes, too much booze, and few lasting relationships. I've had a couple of divorces, and I'm estranged from my kids; success comes with a high price tag. But then I had my breakdown and I, perhaps predictably, turned to drink for comfort.

Mike reckoned I was ground down by seeing too much suffering and senseless violence, lingering conflicts with no apparent goal or purpose. Perhaps he was right. I was continually surrounded by a joyless world with a distinct lack of hope and justice. Anyway, after I got dried out, Mike pulled some strings and found me a position based in Chicago with no foreign travel—a new start and all that. The only trouble now is I'm only doing "human interest" pieces. What a come-down! I'm a hack. If truth be told, however, I shouldn't be trusted with any important stories for a while. Still, I'm back in the newspaper world, so I'm home.

Mike called me out of the blue last week and, after a few pleasantries, he got straight to the point.

"Bill," Mike said, "I want you to go to Goshen, Indiana, and interview an old man called Mervin Hostetler. We are putting together a special edition about Los Angeles. It's been nearly a year since the 'Big One' devastated the city, and we want to celebrate what it once was—a bit of good news and nostalgia, not just doom and gloom. You know the sort of thing that sells well. I've heard some gossip from our Archive Department that this Mervin guy's got an interesting story. I don't know what it is. I don't even know if he is still alive! But I want you to check it out. Oh, by the way, he's Amish!"

And with that he hung up.

"Terrific. What a waste of time and effort!" I said as I slowly put down the phone. "And I'm going to have to do all the leg work myself. Humph, I will probably have to go door-to-door to find this guy, assuming he's still breathing."

Despite the high probability this was a dead lead, I owed Mike big time. Besides, this might be my ticket back to New York.

Mervin, when I finally got to meet him, was not exactly the kind of man I expected. He was, as I did anticipate, typically Amish: grey beard, black trousers, suspenders, and sleeves rolled up on his simple white shirt. His eyes smiled amid his wrinkled face.

I aged him in his late seventies, though his mind was as sharp as a tack. He was expecting me and warmly invited me to sit with him on his deck. His handshake was firm, and under the loose-fitting shirt I sensed the strong arms of a man still used to manual labor.

He called through the open front door: "Sam, please bring an extra glass of cool lemonade for our guest."

Sam turned out to be his granddaughter Samantha. Wow, what a contrast! Her tight jeans, make-up, and loud—but elegant—jewelry caught my eye. Mervin introduced us and told her I was a journalist.

"Bill wants to hear the story, perhaps even write about it," Mervin explained. At this, Samantha became protective of her grandfather and suspicious of me. Mervin sensed this too and tried to calm her with, "Don't worry Sam, God has brought him here."

Oh, dear God, what has Mike got me into? I thought.

Samantha looked directly at me and said, "Don't make Pops out to be a religious weirdo. Do you hear?"

She turned her back on me and walked into the house as I stared on. Moments later, she returned with her own lemonade and plonked herself down beside Mervin, who patted her hand. Samantha then looped her arm through his and smiled at her grandfather. It was clear to me that she was not moving anywhere, so I began my introductory spiel.

It turned out that Mervin was keen to talk, to give me the "full" story, as he put it. I sensed he felt it was somehow important for posterity. I got out my voice recorder, together with my pad of paper and pencil, and listened and took notes for hours. I had never heard such an unlikely—yet enchanting—tale, one that touched my washed-up, cynical heart and one that should be told.

"I was a leader in our small church on Sundays," Mervin explained, "but for the rest of the week I was a hardworking farmer like everybody else. Sure I was young—early-twenties, as I recall—but full of energy and passion about our Amish ways, of our faith, and family values. We were all convinced of our calling by God as a special people, a remnant of faithful believers not wanting to be tarnished by the surrounding culture. We saw the outside world as godless and—frankly—not worthy of redemption. Anyway, one day I was overwhelmed by a completely foreign idea—namely to go to Los Angeles and proclaim to its inhabitants that God was seriously displeased with them. My first reaction was to ignore such a ridiculous thought, as it was an action no Amish person would ever contemplate. I was, of course, passionate about my faith, but I saw it as an *Amish* thing. At that time, I still wasn't even sure about our Mennonite brothers and sisters, thinking that they had sold out on our core values. And what did *I* know of Los Angeles? Very little. I knew of Hollywood's existence, of big universities that promote doubt and anti-Christian education, and of a pleasure-seeking culture. I could not imagine any good thing in L.A. and certainly I was convinced that God *would be* seriously displeased with them. But why me? Los Angeles was half a continent away! But day after day, night after night, I could not shake this crazy idea out of my head.

"'OK God,' I bargained angrily, 'so you want me to go to that evil city and make a fool of myself, telling them what they already know? Well, I simply won't do it and *you* should not be wasting your time on *them*. However, I *will* do something; I will go to India and tell *them* about you. At least they're religious there, and they like men with beards who live simply. I am a farmer, what do I know about concrete cities? L.A. is not for me, but I could do some good for you in India'. I didn't wait to listen to God's reply—I wasn't interested in a conversation.

"In a matter of days I was traveling by Greyhound to New York to find a ship to take me to India. As I sat reading my Bible for comfort, I felt like a fish out of water with people staring at my attire. Moreover, my anger toward God bubbled just underneath the surface. Looking back, I had no idea how I was going to get to India. The whole caper should have been fraught with paperwork and formalities. I was unbelievably naïve and what transpired was probably illegal. But I met some sailors from Indonesia and Sri Lanka who introduced me to their Pakistani captain. 'So you want to tell the Indian people that your God is seriously displeased with them?' he said with a chuckle that I failed to appreciate. 'We've been trying to say similar things for years. Welcome aboard!' The captain must have heard a garbled account of the reason for my voyage, but I did not argue. Everyone was grinning, slapping me on the back and making a fuss as the sailors showed me my bunk. I was to work my passage, initially across the Atlantic, as an odd-job man. They could see from my build that I was used to physical work. Within a few days our container ship left port. I was looking forward to going to India. Los Angeles seemed all behind me now.

"All went well for the first day and I quickly found my sea legs. On day two the ship's radio and radar failed. The captain was very concerned, and engineers worked frantically to try and repair them. News spread throughout the ship that we were electronically blind and some thought this was a bad omen for the voyage. I failed to appreciate its significance, but that breakdown was responsible for us hitting a huge storm which we otherwise would have avoided. The captain was in a mood to match the weather as he tried to guide his ship and valuable cargo through the gale. I helped the crew secure the cargo above and below the main deck. The scrape of metal against metal joined the deafening roar of the winds and waves. Now I have experienced major storms on land—including a tornado—but you are utterly helpless on the high seas—even in a huge ship. The power of God within nature is truly awesome.

"We all went below and waited. However, I sensed the storm growing worse. I could see fear in the eyes of veteran sailors. Some got out their prayer mats. The First Officer burst into the room, 'The forward containers on the top deck are loose; their fastenings must've snapped,' he said. 'Some containers have already gone overboard. What's left needs quickly resecuring. A work party of six should be enough to fix it.' He grabbed a deck of playing cards from the table and gave them a cursory shuffle. 'Highest six cards go. Aces high; be quick now.'

"So, with no choice I was forced into gambling—something that repulses me and I have shunned all my life. Still, as I hesitantly took a card, I reminded myself that the Bible tells us that although the dice is thrown, its every decision is from the Lord.[2] I got the *highest* card, the King of hearts! *God, why me!*

"'The rest of you had better pray,' was the Officer's parting shot as he left to fight his way back towards the bridge.

"Outside, even the secured containers crashed around the rolling deck. We inflated our life vests and attached the safety wires from our chest harnesses to the storm wire that ran the length of the ship. We were all terrified. One false move and you could slip and be crushed. We all knew that we were fighting for our lives and for the life of the ship. We surveyed the problem and secured the forward containers. Progress was slow, but we finally managed it. As we were returning back toward safety, a freak wave caught me unawares and sent me over the side of the ship. I dangled from my safety wire.

"Under normal conditions the other crewmen would have been able to rescue me. But not that night.

"'Cut me loose and save yourselves,' I yelled.

"I saw some frantic activity above me, and moments later a bright orange inflated life raft flew over the side. For what seemed like an eternity, I remained attached to the ship by the wire being battered both by the waves and the ship's hull. Then I remember falling a very long way down into the cold raging waters below.

"Even with a life jacket on, I knew it was it was only a matter of time before I would die. Then I felt a taut wire pulling on me and I realized—between gulps of seawater and air—that I was now tethered to the lifeboat. I pulled on the wire with all my might and slowly began moving toward my only hope of survival. I forgot about the wind and waves and focused all my energies on reaching the orange dinghy. I clambered on board, and once inside its canopy, I zipped up the entrance. I lay panting—bruised, exhausted, and tossed around by the waters. Before long the storm abated, and I dozed on and off until morning.

"The waves were still large the following day, but the rain had stopped. There I was, all alone, in the ocean, in an orange coffin. I shouted at God, 'Okay, so you've stopped me from getting to India, fine. But, out here, I am still not going to L.A! So that makes it one-one, a draw!' God let me stew in my misery all morning until I sensed a large movement in the waters. I stared in horror as an enormous black fin surfaced nearby. I did what sensible people do in the face of certain death: I closed my eyes and began reciting the Lord's Prayer. I said 'Amen' loudly and opened one eye. The fin was still there! Then I saw more movement, and—moments later—heard the sound of a small engine.

I rubbed my eyes and saw six uniformed sailors in a powered dinghy coming towards me to rescue my craft. Within a matter of minutes I was being rushed down a ladder and escorted to a small room which was to become my temporary quarters.

"The officer was formal, but not unkind. After giving my name, he asked if I was a US citizen. I said I was Amish. He paused and smiled. 'Close enough,' he replied, and then he introduced himself.

"After a barrage of further questions he told me that I was safely aboard the U.S.S. Dolphin, a nuclear-powered submarine. It turned out that they had been performing routine manoeuvres and were on their way back to port when they picked up my lifeboat's automatic distress beacon.

"'The commander took pity on you and we picked you up,' the officer explained. 'But although I know you don't pose a threat, you do not have security clearance. So you must remain in here. Have a hot shower. We'll bring some dry clothes and food. And I'll send the doc to look you over. Get some rest.'

"He left, locking the door behind him.

"Later, lying on the bunk, wearing casual Navy attire, I reflected on the irony of this rescue. 'God, I don't like your sense of humour,' I said, 'I am now sealed in an underwater steel tomb. Here I am, a peace-loving pacifist, being saved by an evil war machine. This is an *abomination*! I am even wearing military clothes! What are you playing at? What are you saying?'

"The journey back to port took three days; I wrestled with God and reflected on my enforced predicament. I could get no peace of mind. It was hell."

Mervin paused and closed his eyes.

"That's enough for today," announced Samantha.

"It is," agreed Mervin, "Bill must stay in our guest room and there will be one more for dinner tonight."

And so I got to experience Amish hospitality; there is nothing like it, I discovered. After Mervin said a prayer of thanks for God's provision, everyone tucked into hearty home cooking. There was roast pork, sweet corn, carrots, peas, cabbage, potatoes—and freshly made bread. When I close my eyes now, I can still taste the fresh vegetables and smell the rich gravy.

"You will find the Navy will deny that incidence," Mervin began the next day. "I had to sign various papers to do with 'official secrets.' It was the Cold War, remember, and everyone was nervous. What was I to do? I surrendered; God won. I made my way back home and then took more Greyhounds to California.

"Los Angeles was a disgrace. It was a city of great contrast and nobody shared anything. The rich lived like royalty, and the poor lived in squalor. I was repulsed to see prostitutes and drug dealers on street corners, destitute old men sleeping in cardboard boxes, abandoned buildings covered in multi-coloured graffiti, and trash scattered everywhere. On the beaches, people ate junk food and grabbed pleasure in any way they could get it, oblivious to their nearby neighbors' plight. *There is no sign of justice here; no wonder God is displeased,* I thought.

"'Okay God,' I prayed, 'so what's your message to these people?'

"I got myself a sandwich board and wrote The End is Nigh on one side, and on the reverse, God will destroy L.A. in 40 days. You can imagine the looks I got. What was a young Amish man doing walking around the city looking like a fool? Secretly, though, I was pleased. I *wanted* God to destroy that place. What I saw was an abomination! So I walked around the city with my sandwich board, shouting, 'Repent or perish! You have 40 days before doomsday, so get right with God now while you can.' I didn't want anybody to take up that offer, nor did I expect anyone would. Most people ignored me, some laughed at me. Others thought I was pathetic and looked on me with pity. Several long-haired young people were curious enough to ask how I was sure there were only 40 days left. I even recall being interviewed by a journalist—no doubt just to add some spice to an otherwise dull news day.

"After giving God's warning for three days, which I thought was long enough, I took a bus to the outskirts of the city. I climbed to the top of a large mountain that overlooked the smog-laden valley and I waited. I—somewhat gleefully—wanted to see what happened next.

"After 40 days, Los Angeles was still intact. I was furious with God. 'God, how can I go back to Goshen with any credibility with this evil city still standing? I looked a fool down on the streets and I'll return home appearing an even bigger idiot. Why do you humiliate me like this? I have done what you asked, now is *not* the time to be changing your mind!'

"God spoke to me bluntly and clearly. His words have stayed with me all my life. His tone, in response to my shouting, was commanding and loud. 'What right have you got to tell me what I can and cannot do, or when to act? I rescued you when you were perishing in the ocean. I showed mercy to you when you were unrepentant, why should I not show mercy to others who are repentant?'

"'But God,' I argued, a little more respectfully now, 'these people are not Amish. We have been faithful to you. In stark contrast, this city has had no regard for you or your ways. They deserve your displeasure and judgment.'

"God responded with gentleness and intimacy, 'Mervin, you are special. I know you are dedicated to the simple life - to peace, to family, and to me. But don't let this make you proud. Rather, be delighted that I have used you to bless others. What is wrong with that? Like you, I am concerned about justice, and injustice makes me angry. But I prefer to be gracious, not to punish. To show abounding love and mercy when people respond to me. As you know, if a handful of people had acknowledged me at the time of Sodom and Gomorrah I would have shown mercy; many more have responded to me here in Los Angeles. I want you to go back to your Amish ways with a bigger picture of me and my love. Know that my love crosses boundaries that you do not think possible or appropriate. Know that I can bring good out of evil. Know there will be more people in my Kingdom than you think!'

"What I learned much later was that God used me to speak to some of those long-haired young folk," Mervin continued. "It made them ask questions of God and of themselves that they had not thought about before. Somehow the young people responded to God and many were baptized in the ocean. There were guitars and music around campfires on the beaches, and they began reading the Bible. Basically God poured out his Spirit on many of the young people of L.A. and this was the birth of the Jesus People Movement. Again I sensed God's sense of humor, sending a long-haired, bearded Amish man to reach long-haired, bearded hippies!

"So Bill," concluded Mervin, "I returned back to Goshen still somewhat shamefaced and embarrassed to find that God's Spirit had been working here among individuals as well. God was slowly opening my community's eyes to his larger activity in the world. I spent many months rereading the Bible and being shocked by things I thought I understood. God's love and grace were much bigger and broader than I anticipated."

I am now back in my hotel room, having written up Mervin's story. It seems to offer hope even to someone like me. Perhaps Mervin was right; maybe God really did bring me here to meet Mervin. I'm going to take my draft text back to him tomorrow; I want Mervin to be happy with what I've written. I've never done that for a source before in my life. I must be going soft.

Chapter Three
THE GOD-MAN PROJECT

An Abridged Excerpt from
A Life in Words: An Authorized Biography of God

BY MAX GRAMMATEUS

From the Introduction

I AM A "WRITER," what you might call a heavenly legal secretary. But I'm not just any Writer. I am one of a small group led by Archangel Metatron. It's a great honor to be such a Writer. We chronicle the affairs of the highest Council of Angels whose meetings are chaired by the Maker himself. Not only do we record the official court minutes for these assemblies, but we get to overhear many conversations and comments that remain discreetly unpublished. I love this work. It is for this reason that the Maker encouraged me to translate and publish my living memoir, *A Life in Words,* and relay the atmosphere of the heavenly court as an ongoing journal.

Excited though I am about this project, it is proving problematic. First, you should know something about the Maker. The Maker is a unique identity and, therefore, indescribable in *any* language, even the heavenly language, as words only relate such things as concepts, symbols, and emotions in terms of realities and experiences that are familiar to us. What has been *created* can never fully comprehend the *Creator*. Nevertheless, I will try my best. In doing so, I can only express what the Maker chooses to reveal—and permits me to pass on—to a planet called Earth. Even then I have run into problems, for how can something that is spirit be expressed in language that derives its analogies and metaphors from the physical realm? All mortal languages are blunt tools! Words lack the subtlety, suppleness, and nuance to adequately express the immense richness of the heavenly realm, especially that of the Maker.

For instance, although the Maker is one essence, the Maker is also a united community of love, purpose, and integrity, of three interfused or in-dwelling beings-in-relationship. Even at this foundational point, you can already see a linguistic failure—for how can "three" also be "one"? Should I refer to the Maker with singular or plural personal pronouns: I and my, or we and us? I have to use both. There is inevitably a mystery here. What has been revealed is that these three beings-in-relationship are, in general, never separable. What one knows and feels, the others also know and feel. They were all involved in creation, that's why we angels simply use the term "Maker." Oh, and don't get me started on the matter of gender; that is such a human restriction! Don't forget these language limitations as you read on.

Angels are much simpler to describe because we, like you, are created beings. In fact, we are formed as mature adults. There are no angel babies or children. We will live forever—for once the Maker gives life he does not take it away. Like mortals, we have individuality, free will, and are responsible, relational agents. Unlike humans, we are not classified by race or tongue. We all use the same language. There are various kinds of angels, such as Rulers, Guardians, Watchers, Companions, Messengers, and Warriors. You can see that we are described primarily as functional beings; nevertheless, we know that we have much more value to the Maker beyond what we do.

Angels have a great deal of influence and power to accomplish the tasks the Maker has given us. This strength of ours is where humans are peculiarly weak. What we lack, however, is foresight. We only have a limited ability to imagine what the future might hold. God gave that gift to mortals, and, to some extent, you can shape your future. Human beings might like to have more power to achieve their dreams, while we angels might like to have more insight of future possibilities. But none of us can do anything about that, for that is the way the Maker created us. We are both limited, with strengths and weaknesses. We are simply restricted in different ways.

The affairs in the spiritual and physical realms are discussed periodically at the Grand Council, the highest council of Heaven. Reports from certain heads of angelic departments are routinely given and discussed. In contrast to what I hear about earthly committees, these meetings are far from boring because the Maker himself has exciting and insightful things to say. So there is always an air of expectancy before such assemblies.

The Council Chamber is not used for any other purpose and is decorated lavishly with floating crystals, whose shades and tints are not static, but dynamic, changing their hues to give a sense of a living chamber. Just being in the space fills you with a sense of awe and wonder. The chamber does not seem cold or austere, rather warm and inviting. There is no ceiling. Instead you can see what is best described as choreographed galaxies dancing above. But don't take this image too literally, as we are not that far away from Earth. In fact we are much closer than you imagine. The central feature of the chamber is the large oval table and its chairs, whose design had been specially commissioned for this purpose. The hall exudes grandeur, yet its acoustics—so to speak—sound as intimate as your living room.

As befitting the Grand Council meetings, there is a great deal of pomp and pageantry. This is not done out of the need to impress or to demonstrate self-importance, but simply for the pure enjoyment of all concerned and to celebrate creativity and innovation. The angelic delegates wear brightly colored robes of various styles. But these are nothing compared to the shimmering living colors of the Maker's magnificent cloak. While there is always serious business to discuss at these meetings, the costume and ceremony are the place for frivolity and fun. It heightens the sense of joy and dignity for such auspicious occasions.

At the beginning of one particular Grand Council meeting, everyone stood as the Maker took his place at the head of the large oval table with Archangels Michael and Gabriel at either side. Other angelic dignitaries filled the spaces around the table. We Writers sat quietly in the background to record all that would be said for the official proceedings.

The Maker asked for routine verbal reports from around the table. He is not a micromanager and likes to entrust tasks to both angelic and human agents. The first envoy, Raphael, stood and spoke briefly to the emotional and spiritual mood of the country under discussion.

"I am sad to report that the spirit of the nation is in some disarray. Politics and faith have become confused, with mixed loyalties to those in power and to religious lobby groups who struggle to enhance their influence. There is also a widening gap between the common people and their spiritual leaders, although many such leaders are still widely respected. Out of reverence for traditional texts, some influential people have created extra stipulations and regulations in an unnecessary attempt to ring-fence and protect Scripture. In doing so, however, they have created a burden to those who genuinely seek after you. This has resulted in a spirit of legalism and an emphasis on rules, rather than relationship. The spirit of the nation is therefore disunited, even polarized in parts. The powerless want to take the law into their own hands. In contrast, some of those of high rank are willingly cooperating with unjust political leaders."

The Archangel concluded, "Finally, in these economically difficult times, spiritual thirst is high, but faith and hope levels are low. What they need is a rescuer."

The Maker nodded and thanked Raphael. The floor was then opened for discussion. A few questions were asked from others around the table, but no one found the report surprising; this trend had been noted for a while now.

The second emissary, Jophiel, summarized his report on the social and political scene in the region.

"There have been no major wars for some time now. This peace has enabled a period for repair and construction, for infrastructure development of roads and buildings. The increase in trade and travel, together with human displacement due to war, has resulted in a further mix of cultures, so enhancing ethnic diversity. Even so, there is now a common language that allows people to work together, despite their many differences. Times of peace are, however, problematic for the military, as they prefer a well-defined enemy in order to thrive and maintain their budgets. There are skirmishes from time to time in my geographical area of responsibility. Here the military are present as a peacekeeping force, but with the implied and very real threat to 'behave, or else take the consequences!' Commercial trade is growing, but, as often is the case after an expensive military campaign, taxation is high. Frankly, this situation bodes well for political stability in the medium term, as there are no credible external enemies for this superpower. Even so, localized terrorism and crime remain a niggling issue. Good roads and sailing craft aid communication, and literacy, scholarship, and education are on the increase."

Again the delegates asked more questions and probed as to how confident Jophiel was on his forecast of political stability. The Maker listened. His eyes were smiling at this news.

Several other reports were also heard. As in all committees, details were explored, assumptions and findings challenged. Yet the tone was one of genuine trust and cooperation, of collaborating together for a common purpose within a non-competitive atmosphere.

"Enough," said the Maker calmly, which brought the discussions to a close. "Thank you for your contributions and your diligence in your tasks."

He paused for a moment before continuing what was, as we later discovered, to be an announcement of the most decisive initiative in cosmic history.

"The time is ripe for a new phase in my revelation to my children and for their liberation," the Maker began.

The Maker had the full attention of all the angels. There had been such phases before, as the Maker had previously instigated various plans to restore relationships with his willful creatures. But the whole of heaven had been aware for a time now that something novel was required.

"It is time to be decisive," continued the Maker, "but there also has to be elements of surprise, boldness, irony and uniqueness. Even of mystery. It is the right moment for instigating a completely new way of thinking, while being continuous with the old approach. As you know, the Creation-Project has a purposeful goal, a history with a definitive culmination. But the details are evolving and are being fleshed out in response to how those whom I have given free will choose to act.

"You will recall that what I wanted from the start was a relationship of trust with my children, but the first human generation rejected that offer, preferring total autonomy instead. In time we related with their descendants, Abraham, Sarah, Isaac, Jacob, and their families, and other key saviors emerged, like Joseph and Moses. Lots of new beginnings with good intentions were promised by the emerging chosen nation, elected to reveal our ways to the whole world. Yet even with the guidance of our prophets, people's determined resistance to lasting transformation still proves to be a formidable obstacle. Then, as now, the people do not want a living relationship with me, preferring instead to be similar to those in the world around them. Rather than being a vehicle to bless others and manage creation responsibly, they were seduced by the neighboring cultures and lost their distinctiveness, their identity.

"Of course these difficulties have not arisen in a vacuum," continued the Maker. "The Deceiver has been active twisting our words of life into half-truths. That Trickster has enslaved them, blinded them, and played on their initial innocence to get back at me. Yet the Enemy has limited foresight and, with that weakness, he and his cohorts are severely restricted. All they can do is optimize chaos, wreak havoc, and oppose my values. But they are no equal to me!"

A cheer exploded from Archangel Uriel, who could no longer contain his excitement. Others joined in and applauded; the Maker grinned broadly and shared in their joy.

"Nevertheless," he continued, and the room, full of anticipation, returned to respectful silence, "once I have given free will, I do not override or revoke it.

"As a patient parent, I still want to have a relationship of love.

But my children to this day continue to reject this, imagining they are strong, when in fact they are unaware of their weaknesses. I want to protect them. What I have underestimated is the damage evil does to my children. Their vulnerability and susceptibility were offset by their creative intelligence and curiosity. But that has not proved enough. I have heard their cries for help. I want to take upon myself their suffering, as a good parent would do—if possible—for their children. I am their Maker and know all that can be known about humankind. However, since I am not in fact human, I cannot fully experience their condition. I am unable to truly comprehend mortals."

The Maker paused and added, "Unless I become one of them."

Gasps exploded around the room. This was, frankly, an untenable proposal. The Maker raised one hand to restore order and the room grew quiet.

"I *want* to know. I *need* to know," said the Maker. "Not only does this enable me to experience firsthand the human condition, but it allows me to most fully reveal my character and purposes to them. As I said, it's a distinctive new phase of revelation. Now is the appropriate time, judging by your reports."

The Maker stopped talking to allow the gravity of the proposition to sink in. The angels all started discussing the news with each other, some in excitement and others with grave concern. After a few moments, when the emotional reaction of the envoys had abated, the Maker called for order and invited questions, comments, and requests for clarifications.

One of the delegates asked, "What will the Enemy do? What is your plan?"

"I am One and we are Three, and this has been so from the beginning of beginnings," said the Maker. "In this novel initiative, the God-Son will become human and so become the 'God-

Man.' This is our humbling self-sacrifice for our children. Humankind was made to *reflect* our image; this time an integral element of our identity will actually become mortal. The remaining God-Parent will follow intimately and attentively the life of the God-Man. The dreams and anxieties of parenthood have always been part of our heart, but completely new depths are to be explored in the God-Man project."

"How do you mean to arrive on earth?" asked another angel.

"By being born, of course," replied the Maker with a kind smile, "with a suitably chosen mother, naturally."

The room was already in a state of shock. It would be fair to say that some envoys were close to fainting with this latest news. As a Writer I am privy to the off-the-cuff comments of all the senior angels. Managing the Creation-Project is a delicate affair at the best of times, and consequently some of the emissaries have privately wondered about the Maker's wisdom. The Maker's chosen mode of operation is so self-limiting, so risky, and vulnerable. We don't have the Maker's degree of patience and self-restraint. This latest bombshell seemed to be reckless, endangering the God-Man project from its inception.

"Why can't you just arrive as an adult? Why do you need to undergo the hazards of being born and of childhood?" asked Raphael.

"This is not just for the God-Man's experience, but for the God-Parent too," replied the Maker. "We need to appreciate the full intensity of human vulnerability. Their weakness and fragility we understand 'in theory,' but then we will really *know* and fully comprehend and relate with our children. We also want to further demonstrate the extent of our commitment to them. Arriving as an adult would be inexcusable and prone to criticism. It does not reflect our character. We relate to people of all ages, not just adults, so we need to experience firsthand the normal human development from the very beginning."

The Archangel in charge of the Guardians spoke. "I presume you will want a special protection unit to accompany the God-Man?"

The Maker's response was emphatic, "No, none of that! Just the same degree of protection we give to everyone else."

"But what about the Enemy?" asked the Archangel.

The other angels had a great deal of sympathy, for Guardians had a thankless task. No human appreciates all that they do. Even at this initial stage, being responsible for the God-Man already seemed like a poisoned chalice.

The Maker smiled, knowing what lay behind the question. "I take full responsibility for the project," said the Maker, "but there is still much vital work for you to do."

The Head of the Guardians exhaled and his face relaxed. Relief was also evident in the looks of the other envoys. Having said that, everyone around the table already knew that although the Maker delegated tasks, he always took full responsibility for the whole Creation-Project.

The Maker continued. "This is a war, one that is about to enter a decisive battle. The birth of the God-Man will be a public affair. I am not afraid of the Enemy, so why should I cower away? Public, yes, but not in the way the Deceiver anticipates. It will involve poverty, not privilege. Refugee status, not citizenship. Tradesmen, not scholars or royalty. Furthermore, his mother will suffer ridicule, suspicion, and gossip. She will be falsely perceived as an immoral woman by many. But during the God-Man's adult life, some will revise their views and see her as highly honored. This social tarnishing of his mother will impact the child, as will the role of his human father figure. His childhood will be hard, not luxurious. The God-man will experience all the common domestic, social, economic, and political struggles by being truly embedded within humanity."

Gabriel then spoke up, "How long have you been thinking about this plan?"

"I knew that such a possibility might need to become an actuality from the Creation-Project planning stage," replied the Maker. "Much depended on how humankind would respond to my love, and that I did not know for sure until they had actually decided to reject me. I knew that risk from the very beginning. The precise details have emerged throughout history, as possibilities became actualities. Even so, their hope for a rescuer is engrained within their psyche, but their preconceived ideas will make it hard for them to recognize me."

Michael then said, "Some of the prophets we sent earlier were killed. How do we know they won't do that to you?"

This question was followed by silence. The Maker looked all around the delegates at the table before responding to Michael. "Since darkness abhors light, I fully anticipate that they will."

Pandemonium erupted. It was impossible for us Writers to remain professionally detached. The Maker asked for calm, and, after a short while, silence emerged. Everyone wanted to know more.

The Maker continued, "How else are we to experience the anguish and grief of death unless the God-Man actually dies and unless the God-Parent knows the grief of the loss of the begotten? These are human experiences of which our knowledge is inevitably limited. Part of God's Self will die and another part will grieve. In that way, we will experience both."

Silence reigned around the table while the delegates tried to absorb the magnitude of the shocking news.

Uriel bravely asked, "What will happen after the God-Man dies?"

The Maker leaned back, "For now that remains a secret, even from you, my dearest partners. But trust me. I have a plan! As you know, we have dropped hints, given oracles that can be inferred as foretelling the arrival of the ultimate Rescuer. We have heard the cries of the whole of creation too and the God-Man is entering the domain of the Enemy to recapture it, to reconcile it."

After a short deliberate pause the Maker added, "And we will achieve our objective."

Cheers and applause followed. A sense of excitement now filled the Chamber, replacing the earlier fear and anxiety.

"Come," said the Maker, "let us begin work on the details."

Chapter Four

THE FIRST DAY

DR. CARLOS RODRIGUEZ ARRIVED early in the morning at his office on the university campus. He wanted to make a good impression on the first day of his new academic appointment. Ideally, it would have been better if he had arrived a week earlier to unpack and organize his office before the first semester at his new job began. He had, however, been away for the last month due to a prior commitment. Dr. Rodriguez was exhausted from his trip, hardly the best beginning for the young professor. But he was gifted, focused, and ready for work. Carlos, noticing that his office door was ajar, pushed it open. To his surprise, he found the Head of Department sitting in his swivel chair.

"Ahh, *there* you are, Dr. Rodriguez," said Professor Fred Schuler. "I knew you would be here today and wanted to give you my personal welcome."

He stood up and extended his hand in friendship. Carlos could do nothing but shake it warmly.

"Good to see you *at last*," the Head continued. "*Such* a shame you couldn't have come *earlier*...."

The unfinished sentence hung in the air between them and seemed more than an implied criticism. The Head's directness and demeanor put Carlos on the back foot at that crucial moment of first impressions.

But Carlos recovered well. "Couldn't be helped," he replied

cheerfully, "but now I am here, and I am eager to get to work."

"Good, good," replied Schuler. "Well, once you have taken your coat off, why don't you come to my office. It's just a few doors down, and we can have an introductory chat for a few minutes."

And with that the professor was gone, leaving Carlos stunned. He was well and truly put in his place as the new boy.

About five minutes or so later, Dr. Rodriguez was shown into the Head's office by his secretary. The room was magnificent with a commanding view of the campus. The walls were decorated with his framed degrees and numerous prestigious awards. There were also photographs of Frederick Schuler with certain iconic politicians and world-renowned scholars. The dark oak bookcases were filled, and Carlos recognized many classic works by glancing at their spines. His desk, with leather inlay and overstuffed chair, could not fail to impress. Schuler gestured warmly for Carlos to sit opposite him in a chair, which, although comfortable, was nowhere near as imposing as that of the Head of Department.

Professor Schuler observed Carlos looking over the room—it was, after all, designed to be noticed.

"Impressive, isn't it?" the Head said.

"Indeed it is," Carlos replied.

"It was hard work at the beginning," Schuler said with a hint of reminiscence, "but it has paid off. Who knows, perhaps one day this could be your office."

Carlos sat down and took a good look at his colleague. He was about twenty years older than himself. That is to say about fifty, ruggedly handsome, with a strong jaw line, thick hair—a look that would not be out of place in Hollywood. The professor dressed sharply, as if ready at a moment's notice for a television crew to turn up and ask his opinion on a wide range of issues. Indeed, this was frequently the case, and Schuler was always happy to oblige. Carlos knew of his reputation as a smooth talker and a charmer. No wonder, thought Carlos, politicians wanted to be been with Schuler in public. He made them look good!

Professor Schuler took charge of the conversation. "As I am sure you have ascertained by now," he said, "I have exceeded all the university's expectations for a man of my age—and I still have many more years ahead of me yet! What I sense in you is leadership potential. You're a strategic and original thinker. A man of action and integrity. The department *needs* a new person like that with fresh ideas and drive. But can I offer some kindly advice?"

Schuler lowered his voice. "If you want to quickly make a significant impact in academia, and make your mark on the world stage," he said, "then *I* could be a useful friend and ally. As an eminent scholar, whose views are widely sought, I could provide you with glowing references—thoroughly merited, *of course*—for awards and accolades. I can also suggest your name to international colleagues for invited talks at prestigious conferences. With such things on your résumé, you would inevitably obtain rapid promotion at the university and enhance your own reputation. Wouldn't you like that Carlos?"

Schuler gave the distinct impression that only a fool would pass such an opportunity.

"That is a generous and tempting offer," said Carlos. "However, my interests do not overlap your well-known profile, so I am not sure how significant your help...."

Schuler preempted Carlos' negative-sounding reply.

"I have much *wider* interests—and influence—than you imagine," he said. "I am *sure* we could work together on some aspects of close mutual interest."

"I also value academic independence," Carlos continued. "I know the institution would not want that to be hindered either, or to have my creativity stifled. For my peace of mind, I need to be seen and known as an independent researcher and not as your protégé, covertly or otherwise. If this slows down my academic career, so be it."

Carlos spoke boldly and calmly, yet sweat ran down his ribs from his underarms. This was not a good start to his first day, nor what he had expected.

Professor Schuler looked back at Carlos and thought for a moment before responding. "Carlos, I admire your views. Indeed I remember saying very similar words myself in not dissimilar circumstances." He paused for effect, hoping that even now Dr. Rodriguez might reconsider. Carlos said nothing. "Nevertheless, I am *sure* we will be working together on one thing or another in the future. If you ever reconsider, or want to discuss this matter again, my door is always open."

The professor smiled broadly, showing his perfect, expensive dental work. He stood up and politely ushered Dr. Rodriguez out of his office, but inside his calm exterior he was seething.

Carlos walked back to his office, reflecting on the conversation. Had he been hasty? Could the situation have ended differently? Was there a way to accelerate Carlos' agenda and achieve his objective without compromising the method? No, Carlos concluded, he had no regrets in his response to Head of Department's offer. But he wondered if there would be ramifications to his rejection.

Carlos entered his office and passed many unopened boxes of books and files. Instead of unpacking them, he spent a productive and distracting couple of hours setting up his office computer to the university's various databases. Having obtained relevant passwords, he began to familiarize himself with the software systems.

The telephone rang. It was the Personal Assistant to the university's Research Provost. "Are you free at the moment? Professor Wilson has just had a last minute cancellation in his busy diary and would like to meet with you." Put quite like that, Carlos felt he had little choice but to accept. With the aid of the campus map, he was waiting outside the Provost's suite ten minutes later.

The Provost's P.A., Melanie Sanchez, told Carlos to take a seat. "The Provost will be with you in a moment," she said.

While Carlos waited, he looked at the surroundings. Though modern and different in style, the décor was even more luxurious than that of his Head of Department. He could hardly fail to notice that the personal assistant was beautiful. Carlos looked back at the Provost's closed office door. He noticed the polished brass nameplate—Professor David Wilson—and wondered what was keeping him. Melanie sensed Carlos' discomfort and, eventually, picked up her phone. Moments later she informed him that the Provost was ready to see him now and apologized about the wait. The P.A. then escorted Carlos into the Provost's spacious office, made suitable introductions, and left, closing the heavy door behind her.

Professor Wilson was standing by a picture window that overlooked the campus and the city. Snowcapped mountains loomed in the distance beyond the shimmering lake. He invited Carlos to admire the view. After a few moments of silence, Wilson asked, as if he and Carlos were old friends. "I presume you have repaid your student loans by now?"

Carlos, recalling the expense of graduate school, responded hesitantly, "Yes, just recently."

Wilson simply nodded an acknowledgment.

The Provost moved to the easy chairs that were there for such semi-formal conversations and motioned for Carlos to join him. Carlos sat down and looked around the room. The spotless office made Carlos wonder what work was actually done here. Everything in the office was well-designed, as was the Research Provost himself. David Wilson was about sixty, wore a smart Italian suit and shoes, along with a gold Rolex watch.

"Thank you for coming by at such short notice. I like to extend a warm welcome to all new appointees," the Provost said. "I have looked over your file and see that you have all the makings of an outstanding teacher and educator. *Of course* the university values such skills. But we have to think about your research profile too. If I may, I'd like to encourage you, as you begin your career, to consider the marketability of your research ideas and methodologies. Universities these days are continually seeking to capitalize on commercialization. I sense that some aspects of your proposed activities may easily lend themselves to a profitable enterprise. Naturally, part of the enticement is to ensure that you personally benefit financially from your research. If you work hard at that goal, you will find that the monetary return will quickly eclipse your academic salary. Look at me. My patents and profits from my spin-off companies have made me comfortably rich."

Wilson paused for a moment and then added, "Do you think you can do that, not only for your own long-term career, but for the good of the university?"

Carlos felt uncomfortably cornered again. "Money isn't everything," he ventured. "I didn't become an academic to get rich."

"Of course money *isn't* everything," Wilson said. "I couldn't agree more! But the simple fact is that with a good public sales pitch of your ideas, you *can* become *both* rich and maintain your academic integrity. Just follow in my footsteps, so to speak, but within your own discipline. I'd be more than happy to advise you."

Wilson noted Carlos' idealism and his sensitive conscience. "Remember," Wilson said, "in addition to the societal benefits of your research, the more money you make, the more you can donate to your favorite charitable causes."

"Provost, I appreciate your advice and insight. There are indeed possibilities here," Carlos said. He did not want to offend the Provost, but he had little interest in the commercialization of his work. "I can see that you have been true to your disposition and have notable achievements. I too must I be true to my nature. I am confident that in so doing, my work will result in worthwhile accomplishments that will further enhance the university's reputation."

Professor Wilson considered the reply and realized that the early advantage to his brinkmanship was fading rapidly. Rather then lose face in this opening game of chess, he decided it was better to end the conversation now. The Provost knew there would be plenty of other opportunities to pursue these ideas with Dr. Rodriguez in the future.

Carlos walked back to his office with Professor Wilson's idea preying on his mind. He could see the Provost's logic and he was tired of continually living within a meager budget. Carlos knew that his plans would need sponsorship. But he also knew that he should not abuse his talents and gifts. To do so would jeopardize his long-term vision and personal credibility.

A little later that morning Carlos' telephone rang. He stopped unpacking boxes and answered it cheerfully. Lilith, Professor Schuler's secretary, said there was a Miss Martin to see him. She explained that Miss Martin was enrolled in Carlos' first-year course and had some academic questions. Lilith told him that she would bring the student to his office, along with her transcript for reference.

Ah, a student. This should be straightforward, Dr. Rodriguez thought. Lilith knocked on Carlos' door, briefly introduced the student and handed him Miss Martin's paperwork. Lilith then closed Carlos' office door behind her and smiled to herself as she returned to her desk.

Miss Martin was beautiful and looked older than her twenty years. Her summer tan complemented her flowing dark brown hair. She wore a short skirt, revealing well-toned legs, and a loose-fitting top with a low-scooped neckline. She sat down in the chair, put down her bag, and leaned forward to talk to her teacher.

"Professor Rodriguez, I'm in your first year class and I simply can't fail this course."

"Well, classes don't begin until tomorrow, Miss Martin…"

"My name is Veronica," she interrupted.

"Veronica, don't you think you might be overreacting slightly?" he asked. Poor Carlos, he did not know where to look. Her body was divine, her green eyes were mesmerizing. Veronica's lipstick was the same vivid scarlet as her well-manicured nails. Her delicate perfume was intoxicating.

"You don't understand, sir," Veronica continued. "I have failed this course once already and I need to pass it to complete my degree."

Carlos looked over her transcript and recognized the truth in what she had said. Miss Martin was an above-average student but clearly struggled with this particular topic. Dr. Rodriguez then asked the standard questions. What aspect of the material did she find most challenging? Did she regularly attend class and hand in the assignments on time? How much effort did she honestly put into the course? Did she make good use of the teaching assistants? Veronica gave all the appropriate answers. Carlos, being new, had no basis to doubt her word or sincerity.

Veronica leaned a little closer to Carlos, putting her hand on his desk so that her fingers nearly touched his. Tears began to well in her eyes. "There *must* be some additional things I can do for credit," she said. "I'm prepared to do *anything*."

Carlos recognized what was being offered and slowly stood up, opened his office door and returned to his seat. "It's getting warm in here," he said as casually as he could. "Veronica, my policy is not to make special cases and give extra assignments. I treat all students equitably. I advise you get a private tutor to help you further. I see from your transcript that you are an intelligent student. Approach this course diligently and with a positive attitude. And don't be defeatist before the course has even begun."

Carlos stood up to signify the end of the conversation. "I need to get some lunch now," he added, glancing at his watch. "Veronica you are welcome to come back and discuss the course material as the semester progresses."

Miss Martin recovered her poise and quietly left the room. She grinned to herself as she walked down the corridor.

Dr. Rodriguez went out for some fresh air. He was hungry and thirsty. But he did not want to eat just yet. Carlos wondered for a moment whether he could have gotten away with taking up Veronica's seductive offer. No one need know. Carlos, however, knew affairs were not the right way to behave—and never totally secret. Scandal would ruin his career before it had started. But he acknowledged his vulnerability to her charms.

As Carlos wandered, lost in thought, he passed by an old stone church and went in for some quiet contemplation. Inside, it was dark and cool. Carlos found a pew, sat down, and looked at the stained glass windows for inspiration, comfort, and encouragement.

"Father," he whispered, "it's been an intense, demanding morning—nothing like what I expected! Will it always be like this? If so, I honestly don't know if I can sustain these continual challenges to my integrity."

Carlos heard a familiar voice in his mind: "Son, rest assured the Spirit has been with you all morning helping you respond wisely in all three situations. As you start your new work, know that money, sex, and power are three forceful, insidious, and persuasive temptations to which you, like others, are genuinely susceptible. You are not impervious to these wiles. You *will* face all three again from time to time, but not all at once. Today was a momentous day and you have triumphed. Remember I am always with you. Even so, I want you to go and find some good close friends to help and support you. Companions who will share our vision. Don't look amongst your fellow academics, but seek people from other more ordinary walks of life. They will help you keep your feet on the ground and provide perspective."

After a short pause the voice said, "Just rest here a while."

Carlos closed his eyes and heard a strange combination of distant applause, cheering, and soothing orchestral music. He smiled as he saw glimpses of beings dancing in the aisles all around him. Before long all went quiet. Nevertheless, Carlos felt peaceful, refreshed, and fortified.

It was time for lunch.

Chapter Five

THE SERMON

PASTOR DARRYL WILLIAMS stood up and went to the custom-designed glass lectern to begin his sermon. He looked out over his congregation. Over four thousand were now waiting to hear him preach, most with the expectation that his message had been directly given to him by God specifically for today. As often was the case, Darryl was wearing a patriotic navy blue jacket, a crisp white silk shirt and a bold red tie. His advisors had told him the red tie gave the air of authority and confidence. When your church was this big, every little thing mattered. Nothing was left to chance.

Darryl reflected briefly on how the service had gone so far. It had been excellent. The choir was in good form singing a traditional favorite, so the older folk would be delighted. The worship group was well-rehearsed, creating the appropriate sense of reverence and adoration. He had thought the lead guitarist had been a bit overzealous in one song and the drummer also got carried away, but this would keep the teenagers engaged. That's a difficult age to please. Darryl made a mental note to calm the fears of excess that this exuberance will have triggered in the minds of some of his Elders.

Darryl looked down at the front row. He saw his beautiful wife, Erika, smiling. Their well-behaved two children were already in the Sunday school classes along with all the other kids. It was time to begin.

"Brothers and sisters," said Darryl. As usual, his strong voice was also full of warmth and care, as if he knew each individual there personally. "I am putting aside the topic from the sermon series that I had in mind for today. This is because I feel compelled to speak on one of the well-known parables of our Lord and Savior, that of the Good Samaritan."

The pastor stole a quick glance at George, one of the Senior Elders, who was sitting in a prominent position near the front of the church. George looked puzzled, as Darryl had departed from the script. He should have been speaking on *Spontaneity in the Spirit*, as agreed in the sermon-series planning meeting three months ago.

"Because this parable is so familiar," Darryl continued," I think it has lost its edge, the shock value that the original audience would have experienced. So I want to try and update the story, to make it more alive, more relevant for us today. See what you think."

The pastor relaxed, closed his black leather bound Bible on the transparent lectern. The wireless microphone, virtually invisible alongside his jaw, allowed him to roam around the spacious carpeted platform.

George looked nervous. Pastor Darryl did not know that George had managed to bring along a golfing friend, Congressman Wayne Watson. Wayne somewhat reluctantly agreed to attend with his wife, but did so because it would be good for his campaign. George was unaware of the Congressman's motivation, but nevertheless wanted the service to be impressive and run predictably along well-worn tracks. All George wanted was an encouraging, uplifting hour of professionally and unsurprisingly delivered "church." With a sermon that was slightly challenging, but not too offensive; engaging, but not disturbing. A service with just enough emotion so that you could come away feeling "moved." In the language of James Bond, movies of which George would not admit to watching, a good church service was to leave you "stirred but *not* shaken!"

The pastor began.

"There was a fine Christian young man called Steve who was making a road trip from Denver to Las Vegas. From a heavenly place, so to speak, to a hellish one!"

This raised a few smiles and chuckles in the congregation.

"He was traveling alone in an aging car, not unlike some of the student cars I see in the church car park on a Friday night. The scenery was awe inspiring, as you can imagine, and so Steve took his time. He stopped frequently to hike, camp, swim, and explore God's good creation in this beautiful part of our country.

"Unfortunately, as Steve was driving along in a remote region, his car broke down. To make matters worse there was no cell phone coverage in that area. Now to some people I know, like my kids, a location with no cell phone coverage is a real crisis! But Steve, being a well-prepared hiker, was not concerned. He could survive quite well until a car passed by and he could flag it down for help."

The congregation listened and warmed to the story. Even George relaxed after he saw from the corner of his eye that Congressman Wayne was engaged too.

"The following day, Steve saw a car approaching in the distance," continued Pastor Darryl. "Given the heat, he was pleased that help was at hand. Two young guys got out of their vehicle and approached Steve in a friendly manner. He explained that his car had broken down. Steve, being a trusting sort of person, did not imagine what was about to happen next. The two youths beat him up. They then stole his wallet, camping gear, and anything of value from Steve's belongings. The attackers left him unconscious by the side of the road next to his car.

"Later that day another vehicle came by. It was a large black SUV occupied by a senior politician and his wife and young children on a family vacation."

George blushed and squirmed in his seat.

"They stopped for a moment, at the insistence of his wife. The politician told everyone to wait in the locked SUV while he surveyed the situation. He judged Steve was unconscious, but nevertheless breathing regularly. The man tried to call 911 on his cell phone with, of course, no success. He then looked around. Were they themselves at risk? Were the attackers still close by? If so, what would they do to him—and to his family? He surmised that the situation was dangerous and rushed back to his vehicle. Once inside, the politician started the engine and drove off, explaining his reasoning to his concerned wife. He promised that they would call 911 as soon as they were in a place of cell phone coverage. He convinced himself that, as a good citizen, this planned action would be the best thing they could do for him in the circumstances. However, as their day and journey progressed, they forgot to make the phone call. They were distracted by their family's exciting vacation activities."

George cringed.

"I am *very* sorry about that," George muttered to his friend. The congressman did not acknowledge the comment and continued to listen to what Darryl had to say.

"A few hours later that day a chauffeur-driven limousine came by, occupied by a well-known TV Evangelist."

George's eyes flashed alarm. What on earth was the pastor doing? Surely Darryl knew that developing a television ministry was the next strategic step for their growing church. If not checked, these kinds of attacks on respectable, influential, and wealthy figures would impact the congregation's giving. This kind of foolish rhetoric could undermine the church's finances. He would have to have strong words with Darryl afterward!

"The chauffer stopped the car, got out, and surveyed the situation. He then reported back to the minister, who looked on through the tinted glass window. The TV Evangelist looked at his watch. He was already cutting it fine to make his important speaking engagement as it was. *We can phone 911 when we get back to a more civilized area*, he reasoned. Besides, he did not want to have an injured man bleeding on his white leather seats. Anyway, he persuaded himself easily, it could be dangerous to move him. So the preacher gave his chauffeur instructions to drive on.

"Sometime later that afternoon, a man touring the region on his Harley-Davidson came across Steve. He stopped, took off his helmet, and crouched down to examine the victim. Then he got a bottle from his saddlebag and started to dribble water onto Steve's parched lips. After a while Steve began to stir and moan. He was confused, possibly concussed. His face and arms were bruised, grazed, and caked in dried blood. The fellow traveler, however, felt he had no choice but to risk moving Steve to get him medical attention. So the man gently helped him onto the back of his fully accessorized touring bike. He then carefully took Steve some fair distance and brought him to a hospital.

"The staff there looked over Steve for his ID, which of course was missing. They were therefore in a quandary as to how to treat him, for who would pay? The biker said, 'Here is my credit card. Charge all his expenses to this card and make sure he has a private room and the best of care.' 'Wow,' said the administrator, 'are you sure? This won't be cheap you know!' She then ran a discreet credit check just in case the card was stolen, but it was legitimate. 'That's a mighty *Christian* thing to so, sir,' she added. The biker smiled, 'That's ironic,' he said, 'because I'm a Muslim visiting from Dubai.'"

At that point many in the congregation were stunned, completely blindsided with such a punch line. George's jaw dropped. How could Darryl say such a thing! This was preposterous! How can you make the hero a Muslim?

Darryl, sensing the shock, continued. "Astonishment is precisely the reaction Jesus' hearers would have had when he told the story! Let's think about it together, briefly. This parable was in response to a theologian's loaded question on what he must do to be okay with God. Jesus responds by asking the scholar to remind him what he understands to be the basics. The academic replies, 'To love God and love your neighbor as yourself.' 'Excellent, go and do that,' says Jesus. But the expert, feeling uncomfortable and wanting to make absolutely sure they were talking about the same thing, asked, 'Who exactly is my neighbor?' Jesus replies with the well-known story and ends his parable with, 'So, who of the three people acted in a neighborly way?' The answer was uncomfortably obvious to the theologian, as it is to us today. God wants us to love people with no boundaries. And, especially, to show mercy when they are in need. For example, when disasters happen around the world, we should not be concerned with creed but compassion."

The sound of people shuffling grew louder. Darryl wrapped up his sermon and wondered how many paid attention at the end. A trickle of people left the church in disgust. Darryl could guess why. Some in his church had a poor image of God and a narrow view of God's activity in the world. After all, is it appropriate to respond in a humanitarian way when a tragedy happens if you really believe that such calamities are a part of God's plan or judgment? Or is that somehow acting against God's expressed will? That somewhat fatalistic perspective was not Darryl's own view, but he had heard that kind of sentiment expressed by some Elders. Even the singing at the end of the service seemed forced. After the final blessing, the church cleared faster than usual.

Erika liked to have lunch ready when Darryl came home after a Sunday service. For practical reasons, she and their children always came home separately from Darryl, since his after-service activities and duties were unpredictable. Typically, Erika would feed the children first, who would then go off to play. She would then prepare something special for Darryl and herself. They would eat together and chat about the service. Darryl always valued his wife's insights. Erika realized that today there would be a lot to talk about.

Darryl arrived looking exhausted but otherwise quietly content. He knew he had created some waves, but he had been true to himself and being authentic felt good. Erika was proud of her husband because he had spoken from his heart. His talk had been interesting and engaging, regardless of the reaction. She was hopeful that many of their friends would, on reflection, see the truth in what Darryl had said, even if initially they would be shocked. But Erika was more concerned about the reaction of the Elders.

Over lunch, Darryl told Erika how he felt inspired and relaxed as he retold the parable. Yet he too was concerned there might be a backlash from some of the Elders. Darryl was convinced he had been obedient to the Spirit, and so he was confident the final outcome would be good—once the dust settled.

Later in the afternoon the phone rang. Darryl was being summoned to an urgent meeting of the Board. While no reasons were given, Darryl and Erika both knew that such an unscheduled gathering was unprecedented. Erika kissed her husband at the door. "Be yourself and remember God is with you," she said, giving him an encouraging hug.

Darryl returned home with the news that he had been fired. The Board members had been inundated with comments, texts, emails, and phone calls after the service. They felt the need to respond quickly to this crisis to contain the damage. The Elders—George key among them—resolved among themselves prior to Darryl's arrival that distancing themselves from their pastor was the best way to maintain the unity of their church. Pastor Darryl—though loved by many—was expendable. The Elders asked him to leave, offering an appropriate settlement. Darryl was stunned. He knew there might have been issues, but this seemed a complete overreaction. However nothing he could say would dissuade them.

Later that evening, the telephone rang again and Erika answered it. A few minutes later she came back into the living room smiling. Seeing her joy, Darryl asked, "Who was that?" "You'll never guess. That was Congressman Watson. He and his wife were captivated by your sermon this morning and want to talk further with you. We are invited around for a private dinner with them tomorrow evening!"

Darryl and Erika laughed as they hugged each other. "We'd better get a sitter then!" said Darryl.

Chapter Six

THE JOURNEY

THE REV. DR. I. M. WRIGHT, senior minister of a large, wealthy Toronto church and chairman of the Ontario Ecumenical Council, was frustrated and annoyed—and it showed. He had just finished an afternoon of unscheduled conference calls. It all began with a phone call from the *Globe and Mail*. Apparently they were reporting on a dramatic public "miracle" in the downtown area. "Would Rev. Dr. Wright care to comment?" the reporter asked.

No I wouldn't, thought Martin. *My view would be unprintable!*

However, what Martin actually said was, "Let me investigate the matter further and get back to you."

Martin knew this standard stalling tactic would backfire, because even reputable newspapers can't resist a story that humiliates the Church.

Not long after, his office was inundated with phone calls from concerned ministers and colleagues from various mainline denominations wondering how best to respond. They were urgently seeking an authoritative, unified retort from the Ecumenical Council to denounce this alleged miracle as a publicity stunt. They wanted to create as much distance as possible from these irresponsible religious agitators. All of this fed Martin's busy and bothersome afternoon.

Despite the urgency, denominations struggle to be unified

over what seemed patently obvious to him. But, at long last, the compromise wording of the press release was agreed. The Council members suggested that Martin travel to Ottawa and dispel fears and rumors there amongst religious institutions and national politicians. Normally he would have loved the opportunity to associate with his colleagues and acquaintances, but not in such embarrassing circumstances. Such wild claims of the miraculous went against his modern, rational theology and all that he had tried to foster during his high-profile ministry.

Martin's evening was not getting any better. It was raining and it was rush hour. He had to cancel his other plans for this holiday weekend, and Martin never liked letting people down like that. Moreover, his personal assistant had told him the flights were full, as was the first-class compartment on the train. The Rev. Dr. Wright would therefore need to travel economy class.

This is degrading, thought Martin, as he climbed into a taxi to go to the station. His assistant texted him his reservation number at the Lord Elgin Hotel with a note saying she would send a schedule of tomorrow's appointments later that evening.

The train had just left Union Station and was slowly winding through Toronto's downtown on its way to Ottawa. Kevin was hoping for some time and space to relax, as he was tired from the day's activities and wanted to sleep. But just before the train's departure, another person rushed into the adjacent seat. He couldn't grumble; the train was full. So Kevin put in his earbuds, turned on an iTunes Playlist, and closed his eyes. Kevin hoped the man next to him would get the hint and not disturb him.

Martin, the man who sat next to Kevin, was still flustered. He caught the train at the last minute and their beginning encounter had not gone well. Martin had, none too quietly, forced his luggage into the overhead locker. He mumbled a few choice words as he also tried to wedge his coat into the limited space. As he sat down he nudged Kevin, offering no apology. Martin pulled out a newspaper to read and settled down.

The headlines were all about a woman called Andrea. This person had allegedly healed someone and then preached an impromptu sermon at a large open-air gathering.

"This kind of thing gives the Church a bad name," grumbled Martin in disgust.

Kevin overheard and opened one eye to glance at his neighbor. Martin was still shaking his head as he read through the article. As he turned over the page, he happened to glance at Kevin. Martin then did a quick double take as he stared at a photo on the inside page and then looked again at Kevin. He could barely contain himself.

"Excuse me," Martin said. "Isn't this you in this picture?"

Kevin realized that dozing on this journey was not likely to occur. He was sitting next to someone who apparently liked to talk. He pulled out his ear buds, turned off his music, and sat up before responding.

"Yes, that is me standing by my friends Andrea and Craig," said Kevin.

Martin was, finally, in the presence of someone whom he regarded as part of a growing and dangerous religious sect bent at perverting the faith and misleading people with publicity stunts—like this *supposed* miracle.

People are so desperate for a vibrant spirituality that dramatic experiences always attract excessive attention, thought Martin. He was pleased to be able, at last, to give someone prominent in this new attention-seeking movement a piece of his mind.

"Sorry to disturb you," he said. "My name is Martin Wright, and I am the minister at First Presbyterian here in Toronto."

"Pleased to meet you," the passenger replied with genuine warmth as he shook Martin's hand. "I'm Kevin."

"Were you a part of this…this charade?" asked Martin.

"Yes, I was there—and involved," Kevin said. "But why do you think it was a 'charade'?"

"People are impressionable and gullible when it comes to matters of faith and spirituality. They *want* to believe that miracles *can* occur. It provides hope for the desperate. But we know from science that they don't happen—indeed, they *can't* happen. So it is a cheap trick to have someone claiming a miracle in the crowd, by walking away from a wheelchair, and then to use that as a platform to preach."

Martin was direct and articulate. Kevin knew Martin saw himself as intellectually superior, indeed a cut above in every way.

Martin hadn't finished yet.

"Getting people to come to church is tough these days. Believe me, I know," Martin said. "Our society is less godly than it used to be. My own church is no happy-clappy affair for those who need a spiritual crutch. It is professional, with high-quality music and—if I say so myself—with articulate and carefully crafted sermons informed by the latest scholarship. My strategy is to minister to the elite, since it is they who can change the world. Your kinds of gimmicks are merely an inauthentic display of money-grabbing showmanship that does not help God's earthly cause. I implore you to stop this kind of nonsense."

Kevin scratched his head and wondered how best to reply.

"Martin," he began, "I had been skeptical of the miraculous events I had read about in Scripture and doubted that they occurred quite as they are portrayed. I also wondered if such things were simply folklore or even legends. But then, to my surprise, I witnessed a few miracles for myself. Once that has happened to you, you have no choice but to let such events define your thinking. In my cognitive analysis of what I experienced, I reached the conclusion that a post-rational position was the only option that was defensible. Namely, that miracles *do* occasionally occur, whether I liked it or not."

Most people's jaws would have dropped at this erudite response. Martin himself was startled—but not fazed—by Kevin's reply. While Martin reflected, Kevin continued on.

"In this case, I—like many others—knew of the individual who was healed. He was a person whose legs were paralyzed and who sat daily in the same place begging for money. He had simply fallen through the cracks in the welfare system. Many people will attest to him being no audience plant. Whatever the failings of the *Toronto Star*, their journalists would have easily found out that information. The fact that the event does defy logic and common sense is why it is a newsworthy story."

Kevin sat quiet, waiting for Martin to respond.

"There must be another explanation," said Martin. "For instance, the man could've been acting. We live in an age when we know such things are simply impossible."

"I agree that we need to scrutinize miraculous claims with the best science available to us," Kevin said. "I hope the follow-up story will relate any medical records that might exist. What we deem is 'impossible' is based on our experience. Science formalizes our observations of the regular patterns of nature. I used to think that science actually defined or determined what was possible. But, as I said earlier, once you are confronted with a genuine miracle that defies rational explanation, that event becomes a fixed data point about which your worldview must pivot."

The refreshment cart passed by Martin and Kevin, and they both ordered coffees. Martin also splurged on wine, sandwiches, and a few snacks to keep him going on the four-hour journey. As Martin sipped his hot coffee, he asked what he hoped would be a revealing and incriminating question. "Do you think there are events in Scripture that are portrayed as miracles, but did not actually happen?"

"Of course," Kevin said. "For instance, I don't consider the miracle where 'the sun stood still in the sky' during Joshua's epic battle to have occurred at all.[3] This particular alleged miracle is fascinating for various reasons—not least because it was a point of discussion in Galileo's run-in with the Church. First of all, Joshua commanded the 'sun to stand still.' He should have said 'Lord, please stop the *earth* from rotating!' But never mind the huge scientific or the theological implications of this supposed event for a moment. If it had occurred, it would have had global consequences and so probably would have been recorded in every culture's literature. The Egyptian and the Babylonian civilizations, for instance, were very keen on astronomy and would have noted such a dramatic event. No, taken all together, I don't think this aspect of the story is genuine history. The incident does, however, depict Joshua as having had a victory of legendary proportions and worthy of suitable folklore."

Martin began to revise his opinion of Kevin, and thought he had more sense than he had originally credited him.

"Let me add," Kevin said, "that just because certain miracles most likely did not occur as recorded, it does not follow that *all* scriptural miracles did not occur. I don't think miracles, *per se*, are impossible or to be dismissed as out of hand."

"I understand your line of reasoning," Martin said. "But I don't think the supernatural element to the biblical stories is their real point. Indeed, I think many are simply fictional accounts that try to deify Jesus or give authority to the prophets, in keeping with the mythical literature and expectations of the time. If uneducated people today want to privately view them as historical events, well, to some extent, it does no harm. But their main point is their allegorical or metaphorical meaning. Consider, for example, the stories of Jesus walking on water[4] and calming the storm.[5] No sane person today seriously thinks that they actually happened. The authors were trying to convince people that Jesus was divine. They therefore attribute events to him that common folk would expect a god to be able to perform, such as power over nature. Surely you don't accept such grandiose 'nature miracles'?"

Kevin smiled.

"I agree the style of writing was different in those days," he said. "I can't deny that it is possible that an author embellished some incidents to serve his literary purposes. They were certainly selective in what incidents they reported. But is not the same also true today? No one can report 'facts' impartially, with the absence of an agenda. Even the choice of which facts *to* present introduces a bias. We all have our own perspective of what we presume to be important, let alone a prejudice that may be due to a sponsor, what will sell, what is politically correct, and, not least, our underlying philosophy or worldview. None of us is value-free, or unbiased, and we need to examine critically the foundation from which we assess those narratives."

Martin listened as he began to eat his sandwich.

"Having said that," Kevin said, "I *do* believe the 'walking on water' incident to have actually occurred. Why? For several reasons. First, several Gospel writers record it—each with their own distinctive audiences in mind. Second, I agree that it may be true that up-selling the events by adding supernatural elements could convince the uneducated of a connection with the divine.

But that would hardly impress the Greek-educated intellectual elite. How, ultimately, does that help feed the long-term spread and durability of a new religious movement? Convincing the educated and influential is critically important. Moreover, I think we do a disservice to think people in antiquity were ignorant of nature just because they could not articulate their observations in the scientific ways we do now. They knew that walking on water was unnatural. After all, the lake didn't just freeze over! We view them as simple minded and gullible, with the confident rejoinder that we are neither! Third, if we assume—as we sophisticates tend to do—that the people back then were educationally backward, how does interpreting such events as figuratively help? Symbolism, metaphor, and allegory are for thinkers, not the simpleminded. Instead of your suggestion that the nature miracles are merely a literary device, what if they were reported because they were myths that *actually* happened. That was their distinction. That was their shock value. Their significance was self-explanatory. Obviously, such events are outside of anyone's expectation, whether or not we live in an age of science. All such things can only be seen with the eyes of faith, of course. But if Jesus did walk on water, what is the *theological* reason? Surely that is the key issue."

The Rev. Dr. Wright was not happy because he had assumed the only logical explanation for the news story was that the so-called miracle had been fraudulent. He expected the people involved to be Bible-bashing weirdoes, as he had come across this kind of thing before. People, like Pooh-Bear, with "very little brain." Folks who shun all reasoned argument and scholarship, and who simply cling on by faith, regardless. Kevin was not what he had expected. Of course, he could debate the issue, and, indeed, he planned to do just that. But he could not simply dismiss the matter as he had originally anticipated.

"Go on," Martin said as he continued to eat.

"The Gospel miracles were signs of the presence of the kingdom, or reign, of God. Of God's rule here on earth being inaugurated by the long expected Messiah, Jesus, in a new way. He taught as one with authority, something at which everyone marveled. His teaching was backed up by extraordinary, miraculous acts as signs pointing to his identity. With the benefit of hindsight, the authors saw such deeds as fulfillment of prophetic expectations. As you know, the ancients regarded water as the embodiment of chaos over which God instills order in his creative acts. We have other stories depicting water as being associated with the forces of evil, such as the Red Sea incident and Jonah being thrown overboard in the storm. In John the Seer's futuristic vision, the New Heaven and New Earth will have no sea, signifying that chaos and evil have finally been overcome. What better way to illustrate this but for Jesus to actually walk on water and for a fierce storm to be calmed! Graphic miracles that, I grant you, *are* full of allegory and symbolism. But ones remembered because they actually took place. We can have all the theological and scientific expectations we like, but when a new experimental observation arises that challenges the status quo, then we have to rethink our starting assumptions. That is how both science and religion move to new paradigms. Just as Copernicus changed the way astronomers viewed the cosmos, Jesus is the data point that defines the new Christian paradigm."

Martin had heard such arguments before and dismissed them out of his prior commitment to modernism, the spectacles through which he viewed all such events. Martin had not fully come to terms with postmodernism, although there were elements he did embrace. But he was still wrestling with the implications of such a broad philosophy, one that defies definition, and with—as he saw it—its potential danger of sliding into relativistic meaninglessness. Moreover, he did not like the prospect that postmodernism could not rigorously rebut Kevin's perspective. Yet, this was the closest that Martin had been to someone who claimed to have seen a miracle. It was, he thought, perhaps a providential opportunity to investigate such things further. He sat back and began to sip his wine, which tasted marginally better than he feared.

"Tell me," Martin began, "you said earlier that you too doubted the miraculous until you witnessed some events for yourself first hand. These experiences forced you to move *beyond* reason—as you put it. I'd be interested to hear more about that."

So Kevin began to recount his experiences, including his face-to-face encounter with the risen Jesus, as the train journeyed through the night towards Ottawa.

Chapter Seven

THE NIGHTMARE

WHATEVER YOU MAY THINK of Pentecostal preachers, you can't say that they fail to be passionate about the gospel. They are known to be excitable, challenging, unsubtle, and loud. And Pastor Lloyd was no exception. His muscular physique only added to his commanding charisma as a gifted leader and a powerful preacher. No wonder he was nicknamed "Rocky." Lloyd Fisher was the senior pastor at an Assemblies of God megachurch in San Francisco and the national superintendent of the denomination. People flocked to hear his dynamic and compelling preaching, but also in the hope that they might be healed. A number *were* genuinely healed. Surely that's not a surprise if Pastor Lloyd was truly a man of God—which he was. Whether we like it or not, God seems to use some strange people and methods to advance his purposes.

As part of his duties as national superintendent, Lloyd made periodic visits abroad to encourage other Pentecostal churches around the world. He, together with a support team of six, had just finished a speaking tour of some of the major cities of Australia. They were now in Singapore on the return leg of the trip, one which included Bangkok, Hanoi, and Hong Kong. Lloyd was particularly excited to visit this strategic, multicultural city where East meets West.

The pastor and his team stayed in a luxurious mansion.

Ethan, a local entrepreneur who had recently become a follower of Jesus, had offered to put them up in his home. The surroundings were so lavish that some in the visiting team were concerned as to the legality of Ethan's business. They graciously kept their doubts to themselves, which was probably just as well, and praised the Lord for his provision!

Pastor Lloyd was very tired from his busy schedule in Australia. He was looking forward to a few days rest in Singapore and seeing the sights for the first time. But having only recently arrived, he went for a mid-afternoon rest and fell into a very deep sleep.

As he slept, he dreamt of a huge diamond-shaped marquee that—he realized—was aligned with the four points of the compass. Under the white canopy he saw a very large and joyful party in full swing. He noticed that the people were from all over the world, as many were wearing traditional national dress. He then saw nuns, priests, and ministers, all recognizable by their clerical robes, laughing, as if sharing a joke. He observed, with some misgivings, that some were obviously drinking champagne while others celebrated by smoking cigars. There was lively music and food to satisfy all culinary tastes. It dawned on Lloyd that people were not in national or denominational cliques but were mingling together in genuine enjoyment of each other's company. Pastor Lloyd was repulsed, as he feared he had gate-crashed a multi-faith gathering. He then heard a voice he instinctively knew was Jesus saying, "Lloyd, welcome! Come and join the party."

The whole celebration became silent and everyone turned to look at the new arrival. He then saw Jesus standing next to a head-shaved man in a bright orange robe. The pastor shook his head in shocked disbelief. He blurted out, "No way! I can't believe what I am seeing. I have never associated with such people!"

Jesus moved toward Lloyd and replied, "Don't judge. You

are only seeing the outside, but I know their hearts and their actions. Do not turn away from those whom God has forgiven."

It was all too much for Pastor Lloyd. He woke up in a sweat, relieved that it was just a bad dream. What he needed was a calming brandy or a stiff whiskey. Alas, as a principled teetotaller, that option was out of the question. The pastor got up and splashed his face with cold water in the large, spotless washroom. Lloyd still felt exhausted, so he lay down again and promptly fell back to sleep.

He had the very same dream again.

And then again!

Pastor Lloyd knew his Bible—well, at least the bits he had underlined. He realized that having the same dream *three* times was not mere chance, but was significant. Had not Samuel been called three times by God while he was sleeping? Jesus was dead for three days before the resurrection and the Apostle Peter had denied Jesus three times. Pastor Lloyd knew that the number three signified emphasis. Those biblical incidents were important, they unequivocally happened. This dream, Lloyd reasoned, was somehow of great consequence. But he dreaded to think why. What could this nightmare mean?

As Pastor Lloyd pondered, three people arrived at the gate of Ethan's mansion. They explained to the security guard that they had come all the way from Kuala Lumpur to this specific address to speak to a man called Lloyd Fisher. The security guard was suspicious, thinking that they might be con-men, even though one of them was wearing a military uniform with a blue beret and United Nations insignia. The visitors did not help their cause when they explained that they knew a man called Ethan lived at this house, because a messenger from the heavens had told their boss the address. However, the security guard knew Ethan was entertaining visitors and so phoned up to the main house for advice.

Meanwhile, Lloyd's troubling afternoon took a new turn. The pastor was trying to get his head around the meaning of his dream, when he recognized the familiar voice of the Holy Spirit speaking to him.

"Lloyd," the Spirit said, "three people are waiting at the gate to meet you. They will ask you to visit their superior in Kuala Lumpur. Do not think twice about going with them, because I have sent them."

Lloyd was already confused enough and wondered what God was saying and doing, but he knew he would be obedient. After all, the only way to resolve this mystery was to press forward and see what transpired.

Before long, the three visitors were welcomed into Ethan's home. They told Lloyd and his team their story.

"My commanding officer," began the man in the uniform, "is Colonel Perwira Megat of the U.N. Peacekeeping Corps. We work in the Timor region, but right now our unit is on a period of rest and relaxation at our headquarters in Kuala Lumpur. Our colonel is an honorable man and serves the Holy One. He is known for his compassion and generosity to the poor, regardless of their nationality. While he was meditating yesterday, he saw what he described as 'a messenger from the Transcendent One.' The messenger said, 'Perwira, I know your heart and have noticed your good deeds. They are as fragrant incense to me. Send word to a man called Lloyd Fisher visiting from America. He is staying at the home of Ethan Tanner, whose address I will shortly give. Invite him to your home and listen to what he has to say.' We have therefore followed our orders and all the details that the messenger gave have been astonishingly accurate. We therefore invite you to come and experience the hospitality of our Colonel and his family."

When Pastor Lloyd and his team arrived in Kuala Lumpur, they were shocked at the large reception committee in Colonel Megat's home. In addition to his large family, a group of his friends welcomed him. They came from various cultural backgrounds. A number were in military attire and others wore colorful ethnic dress. They were all joyful but stood at attention to meet Lloyd and his party, who, they reckoned, must be very special people indeed. The colonel, in full military uniform displaying various medals, took off his beret and knelt at the pastor's feet. "We are honored and humbled by your presence, sir," he said.

Lloyd was horrified. "Get up, *please*," Lloyd said. "I am only a man like you."

Perwira, blushing and somewhat confused, rose to his feet.

"I am truly out of my comfort zone by being in your home. I have never been in the home of a pagan before, and I am not sure what my church back home will think of me by visiting you. However, God told me back in Singapore that I should not call anyone profane or unclean."

This tactless, arrogant opening remark by the American pastor should have created an international incident that would take a small team of diplomats to resolve. Amazingly, the hosts simply smiled patiently and then graciously offered Lloyd and his companions delicious food and refreshing drinks after their journey. Once everyone was comfortable, the colonel reiterated his story about the messenger. He ended his impassioned speech with, "So thank you for coming and we are all eager to hear what the Holy One has commanded you to say."

They all waited.

The pastor was stunned and initially said nothing. The Holy Spirit hadn't given him a *message*, as such. All he had said was "Don't hesitate to visit Kuala Lumpur." Lloyd looked at his team members who were all equally baffled. They shrugged their shoulders. Lloyd, seeing the diverse colourful attire and nationalities in the room, suddenly remembered his nightmare. Things started to click into place in his mind and he remembered the words Jesus said. After a long embarrassing pause, Lloyd spoke as if he were thinking out loud.

"Now I understand that God has no favorites," Lloyd said. "But in every nation, anyone who honors him and does what is right is acceptable to him."[6]

Lloyd continued with what anyone who knew him would expect: a fiery sermon. But before he had even got warmed up, something shocking happened. The hosts and their visitors all began speaking in tongues. Some languages were human, others seemed angelic. Lloyd and his team starred in bewilderment. They could comprehend and interpret some of what was being said, and so understand that they were glorifying the Creator God. The pastor recognized that this was the Holy Spirit at work. But this was out of order! For none of the host party had even mentioned the word "Jesus" or "Christ," let alone make anything like a confession of Christian faith.

God, what is going on? Lloyd prayed.

"Lloyd, relax!" God replied. "I am at work in them and in you. Do you think that my Spirit works only through people with similar views to your own? Open your eyes to others who are working to bring about my Kingdom. The Spirit is like the wind, you have no monopoly on his activities. We listen and respond to all those who call out to us. Of course, people can only know me through the actions of my son, Jesus. But there are many ways to Jesus."

Pastor Lloyd looked at his six American colleagues and said, "We know the Spirit is at work here. We have no choice but to baptize them and welcome them into God's family." And so they did. And there was much merriment and excitement. Then some of the Lloyd's team stayed several days.

Pastor Lloyd was deep in thought as he traveled back to Singapore for his next series of planned engagements. He could hardly believe, let alone comprehend, all that had transpired. Lloyd's mind began to race through the many non-Jewish characters within the Old Testament whom God used to forward his agenda. People like the Egyptian princess who saved Moses, Moses' father-in-law Jethro, Rahab the prostitute, Ruth from Moab, the Persian King Cyrus, and many others who were also outside of the covenant. Why had he not recognized before that God was at work in their lives too? He promised himself to study these people afresh as a matter of urgency.

Lloyd's mind moved on to other concerns. What on earth would he report back to the denomination's General Meeting? What would he say to his home church Elders and congregation? What he had witnessed went against all that he had previously believed. But the pastor could not deny his experience in Ethan's house or that in the colonel's home. He realized this incident would demand an instant revision and broadening of their mission policy. Lloyd also guessed that the church would be dealing with the practical consequences of such changes for years to come. He wasn't looking forward to going back home to the States, as the responsibility for instigating such changes would rest on his shoulders.

Still, I'll just have to do what I've always done, he thought. *And tell it how it is.*

Chapter Eight
THE AUDIENCE

"LADIES AND GENTLEMEN," the interviewer said, "please give a warm welcome to our honored guest this evening. Live, by special satellite link, the Reverend Paul DeTarsus!" The people in the crowded auditorium applauded as if Paul were a Hollywood celebrity. This made Paul uncomfortable, since he was not used to this kind of reception. Paul was "attending" the annual *Christian Leadership Conference* in Atlanta, a prestigious high-profile event that was translated and beamed by closed satellite link to many locations around the world. It was rumored that even the Pope and the Archbishop of Canterbury had envoys, if not in person, privately watching the event. The conference itself was structured into various independent sessions and designed to foster leadership within the Church, as well as encourage business leaders to seek more holistic and ethical policies within their companies. Some of the sessions had been inspiring talks by secular motivational speakers. Others were overtly Christian, with nationally known speakers and authors. Some sessions had been specially recorded one-on-one interviews with a notable political leader, or an internationally renowned social activist. This particular satellite interview was a unique coup for the conference organizers.

The host continued: "Paul DeTarsus has led a dramatic life as a missionary-theologian, travelling and establishing a string of small churches. He has been arrested, imprisoned, shipwrecked, and has even experienced execution attempts on his life. Moreover, Paul had a major falling out with Pope Peter I. He is an influential leader, a prolific letter writer, some of which are published and well-circulated."

Indeed, many in the audience were familiar with Paul's correspondence; others were genuinely impressed by that brief résumé. Even if you weren't a Christian, Paul sounded controversial and hence, by definition, interesting. After all, if Rev. DeTarsus had been in trouble with both the Pope and the secular authorities, he couldn't be all bad!

"Paul? May I call you that?" asked Liam, the interviewer, whose joy at the prospect of interviewing Paul was barely containable.

Paul smiled and nodded his assent.

"Paul, I have to say this at the outset, you have managed to tick off a lot of women with your rhetoric. Even my wife, who is no feminist, is annoyed! You wrote, and I quote, 'Wives submit yourselves to your husbands…' or, more simply, 'Wives obey your husbands.'"[7] Liam, speaking to the live audience (and into the camera), quipped, "Now you can see why she is infuriated!"

This wisecrack resulted, predictably, in masculine chuckles and polite applause from the audience.

"Actually, Liam," replied Paul with a grin, "I know that comment is widely attributed to me. But the truth is I did not write that particular letter, although I know it is commonly thought to be one of mine. Another close colleague, though more socially conservative than myself, wrote that viewpoint. What I *did* write though was this: 'Your gender, ethnicity, and social standing are all irrelevant when it comes to Jesus.'[8] So I hope that might go some way to addressing your wife's legitimate concerns about me. In fact, the practical consequence of my own statement is what got me into trouble with the Pope!"

"Really!" exclaimed Liam, "tell us more."

"Not a lot to tell, actually," said Paul. "Theologians can passionately and loudly disagree. In this case it was a face-to-face meeting, more like a nose-to-nose shouting match, if truth were told![9] But I remain so convinced that I was right. The issue was not about gender, but race. Christianity is for all races, not just for white people. The same is also true for Christian leadership and scholarship, by the way. Pope Peter agreed with me in principle, but in practice he demonstrated a veneer-thin layer of acceptance that covered a racist's heart. A person's mind and heart have to be truly united against racism. Moreover, Pope Peter should know that God has no favorites. So I challenged him to stop sitting on the fence, to stand up, and actively lead the Church through this contentious issue."

"So how do you get on with Pope Peter now?" asked Liam, seeking an indiscreet response.

"Let's just say we have mutual respect—and we keep a fair distance apart!" Paul said with a mischievous twinkle in his eyes.

The audience roared with laughter. They knew firsthand that genuine leaders often struggle to work closely with other leaders.

"Going back to your letters, how do you feel about the way people have treated what you wrote all those years ago? Are you flattered? Surprised? Frustrated?"

"To be totally honest," replied Paul, "I am dumbfounded that my letters became viewed as authoritative for the worldwide community of Christians. Never in my wildest dreams did I think that they would be collected, published, translated, and scrutinized. If I had known, I would have been far more careful and precise in what I wrote! So, yes, I am somewhat flattered. But I am also shocked and dismayed the way some have used my writings—and those attributed to me—to justify, for example, slavery, anti-Semitism, and patriarchy, resulting in the abuse, persecution, and domination of others. I simply despair at the various ways certain words of mine have been distorted and taken out of context. More positively, however, I am thrilled that my letter to the church in Rome, in particular, has inspired the development and reform of Christ's church and its theology over the years."

"If you were able to be here in person, or write something new, or communicate through some other means, what would you want to say *today*?" asked Liam. "Would your message be different?"

"Wow, Liam, what a great question!" Paul said with a sense of glee at that prospect. "As you know, my letters were originally to churches. So I would especially want to communicate to church leaders, but with their congregations and wider communities looking over their shoulders, so to speak. With that kind of transparency, everyone could hold leaders accountable. That is why I am thrilled God has granted me this opportunity to address your conference."

"Well, we are equally honored—but what would you say?" pressed Liam.

"First, I am disheartened by the lack of unity in the worldwide Church, especially within Protestantism with its proliferation of denominations. That a portion of this disunity can be traced back to different interpretations over my own writings only adds personal insult to injury. Schism is the last thing I want. I have strived to maintain unity within inevitable diversity.

"As you know, a computer is made up of many components," continued Paul, "all of them are essential and all must work together to function properly. It requires a central processor, memory, a hard drive, a visual display, a keyboard, a power supply, and—of course—Wi-Fi. Where would we be without Wi-Fi?" The audience laughed and Paul knew he held their attention.

"What would happen if the hard drive were jealous of the faster speed of the memory, or the display too vain to be associated with the ugly wiring, or if the cooling fan wanted a more exalted role? What if the processor was too proud and proclaimed, 'I am the brains of this outfit and I don't need you!' You can see that all it takes is just one element to refuse to cooperate and the whole computer would not function. Every part *needs* every other part. For Christians to be different is not only acceptable but to be *expected* and *necessary* for the richness, wholeness and vigor of Christ's church—the family of God."

Liam smiled and politely held up his hand to stop Paul from going on. "Preachers!" Liam joked with the audience. "We are passionate people. Once we start we're hard to shut up!"

The conference attendees laughed, yet quieted quickly, as they were intrigued. Many had families where various members were divided by denominations, and this issue, it was simply baffling and off-putting to those unchurched.

"Don't you think that differences in social status, wealth, race, and religious and ideological backgrounds and aspirations are simply a normal part of our human existence?" Liam asked. "Won't this inevitably result in diverse styles and forms of worship?"

"True enough," Paul said. "I recognize the need for different expressions of worship, including communities based around language and ethnicity within a multicultural setting. That is an inevitable consequence of the growth of the Church. And you can imagine that I am always thrilled about church growth, both horizontally and vertically! Horizontal growth builds relationships and community, and vertical growth produces real spiritual depth in communion with God. What I oppose, though, is theological diversity on the essentials. For that is genuine schism and it undermines *Christ's* church. God's family is to be *one*. Whatever our disagreements, we should never lose sight of the fact that what unites us is far more important."

Liam saw an opportunity for clarity on the "essentials" of the Christian faith, or the "fundamentals" as he would have preferred to express it. So Liam asked Paul to explain what he meant. Paul, like a seasoned politician, didn't answer the interviewer's question directly. His wisdom as a leader naturally guided him to make the point he himself wanted to emphasize.

"Our baptism unites us," Paul said. "Baptism's an old-fashioned word, I know, but one full of life-giving symbolism. Baptism is a traditional washing ritual that outwardly acknowledges our Maker's unconditional acceptance of us and embraces us into Jesus' visible family, the Church. As we reflect honestly on our lives, we are all aware of our regrets, weaknesses, and sense of failure and shame. Others may live with a sense of meaninglessness, wondering if anything ultimately matters. We can brush these unsettling thoughts aside temporarily, but they weigh us down—like an anchor—impeding our becoming. They can even enslave us in bondage of various kinds that rob us of the full potential of life. The kind of outward-looking fulfillment our loving Creator wants us to experience and know. What we dream of is a new beginning—but not just that. We want hope that this time it really will be genuinely different and we can leave the negative things of the past behind. We want not just to be released from our prison, but desperately crave an empowering new meaning-making identity. The modern lie of individualism tells us we can do this on our own, but we can't. In part, we need a community that will accept us regardless of our past or status or gender or race. A community that sees me as I can become, not as I once was, and where we can all walk humbly together in becoming all we can be. A new society where shame and guilt are forgotten, overwhelmed by love. Jesus' family, of which we are a part through baptism, *is* that parallel society—*within* our culture but not *of* it. Remember, this is *Christ's* church—not Luther's or Calvin's or Wesley's or the Pope's or that of any other charismatic leader. Regardless of what we think or feel, we *are* united simply because of baptism."

Liam smiled to himself as he had now experienced Paul's passion for preaching firsthand, something he had secretly longed for all his life. Yet he was also confused. Liam already had a firm impression of what Paul would be like, deduced from Paul's own letters and supplemented by an account of his life that Liam had read. But Paul's words sounded to Liam more like what he imagined an evangelical Catholic to proclaim, and that was a bit disconcerting. Still, Liam knew this candor was precisely what the *Christian Leadership Conference* organizers had hoped for in their keynote speaker. Liam, being the professional minister that he was, allowed Paul the freedom to continue. Liam knew that if he interrupted Paul too much, he would be seen as too controlling or manipulating an interviewer. Best to let the charismatic speaker say his mind. Liam knew this session would be devoured afterward. Besides, Paul was the star attraction.

"Returning to Christ's church as the computer metaphor for a moment," Paul continued. "We, the computer components, all have a place and a role within the computer given to us by the Spirit of Jesus. These different functions have been given by the same Spirit for the benefit of every part. Consequently, these varied roles are not to be a source of distinction or division, but to enhance the life of the whole community. But the Church, like a computer, is more than just the sum of its components. It needs the Spirit of the Maker to breathe *life* into it, to *empower* it—and baptism does that too! This Spirit is like the operating system that communicates and interconnects the computer's hardware. Without the Spirit, the Church is lifeless. With the Spirit there is vitality, so enabling the computer to fulfill the Maker's purposes. As each person plays their part, the Church matures in Jesus-like qualities, such as love, joy, and peace. And add to those virtues, patience, kindness, goodness, faithfulness, gentleness, and self-control."

Paul paused for a moment, and Liam interjected a summary: "So, your vision, then, is for a community where the Spirit's life is evident for the benefit of all, where everyone is indispensable, and where difference is celebrated."

"Precisely," Paul said. "Remember that such unity is also at the heart of the Trinitarian God. Consequently, if we—the Church—claim to reflect something of God's nature, then squabbles and factions that then lead to schisms *must* be addressed and resolved."

Then the camera zoomed in on Paul's leather-worn face and whose crow's feet made his eyes joyfully alive. "Leaders," Paul continued, "work tirelessly for healing and reconciliation. For a watching world is waiting for behavior that is coherent with our message. A healthy church will be like a light in darkness, evident and attractive as a living witness to what only God can do in our world of estrangement, discrimination, and fear."

Since Paul had made a contrasting connection between the Church and the world, Liam used the opportunity to casually invite Paul to expand on his insights on Western culture.

"I was given a special dispensation to view some of your TV programs in preparation for today," Paul said. "What I have seen compels me to say that elements of your culture are shallow and escapist. You trivialize and revel in sex and violence, not dissimilar to my own world. You seek wisdom from celebrities, so-called 'experts', and pundits of all kinds. It seems to me that in a world of charlatans and cosmetic surgery, you crave authenticity—the real deal.

"Some look for wisdom, others demand rigorous proof, many crave mystical experiences, but I simply proclaim Jesus who was killed by humankind. But God said 'NO' and raised Jesus back to life from the dead. Foolishness, impossible, counter-intuitive? Yes! But the one who nevertheless has turned world history upside down. Don't trip over this gem of truth! And remember the lack of retaliation of the resurrected Jesus is consistent with his non-violent message of 'love your enemies.' Instead of revenge, he responded with compassion and forgiveness."

Paul leaned forward towards the camera, his body language expressing earnestness. "Jesus even forgave me. So I know now that love is the better way. But what is love? Love is not sex or sentimentality. It is not a warm fuzzy feeling, fluffy, or weak. You can have all the academic degrees in the world, be the greatest philanthropist, be a martyr for a noble cause, or a spiritual guru, but without this thing called love all these good things are garbage. Love seeks the best, not the worst, wants to build up, not to tear down. It is self-giving, not self-seeking. Love is an action, a commitment, strong, and dependable. Love lasts. Experiences come and go, wisdom is contextual, knowledge is relative, but love endures forever."

Liam, right on cue, said, "Paul, you are noted for saying 'faith, hope, and love remain, and the greatest of these three is love.'[10] You have already spoken about love and faith, would you comment more on hope?"

"I have observed that people today put their hope in various things, such as in wealth, education, welfare, scientists, and lobby groups. For others it is in the medical profession, the justice system, politicians and their parties, or in the creativity and the resilience of the human spirit. But my hope is in the faithfulness of God. God is a God who keeps his promises."

Paul paused, and then said, "And now I have a confession to make."

"Really," Liam said, leaning in towards Paul.

"I was wrong in my conviction concerning an imminent *parousia*, by that I mean the second arrival or presence of Jesus. I genuinely thought that event would occur within my lifetime, but I was mistaken. It is healthy for Christian leaders to admit their mistakes. Even so, my hope—and, I trust, your hope—continues to be in the faithfulness of God. And because of that, I want to emphasize the following: To those who are old, sick, or dying, or who have loved ones who have died—take heart! When you see the first blossom on a tree after a long, hard winter you know spring is definitely going to happen. Jesus' coming back to life after his death is like that first blossom. And what happened to him will also happen to all those whom Jesus deems to be his own, including you and me. Moreover, just as his resurrection body had a new physicality—discontinuous, yet continuous with our present reality—so our frail bodies will be renewed in unimaginable ways. There is a mystery here, I fully admit that, but our hope is in the faithfulness of God and the power of the resurrection. Smell the sweet fragrance of that blossom; focus on its beauty! And remember, whether we die from a freak accident, a natural disaster, cancer, in battle, or from old age, we can never be separated from the love of God, demonstrated for us in Jesus. Therefore, be free from the anxiety of the finality of death.

"But there is even more to our hope! Creation itself, like our aging bodies, groans for renewal. Humankind is an integral part of God's good creation. So if God will restore us, will not God also heal the entire cosmos? Of course God will! God remains committed to the world in long-suffering love.[11] The resurrection of Jesus demonstrates the Creator's power and commitment to the whole created order. God is ever patient. His timing for the *parousia* remains an unfathomable mystery. But God will never abandon us. Our great Christian hope is ultimately for a renewed earth; a new creation metaphorically birthed from the old one. Don't get bogged down with scientific questions of 'how'? Instead hold on firmly to the faithfulness of God.

"In the meantime, live by faith, not certainty. Hope, not finality. Love, not power.[12] Because you can count on God to finish what God has begun, persevere in all goodness. Don't be ashamed of Jesus, for he is the power and wisdom of God revealed to the world. Don't be embarrassed by the weirdness of his good news message either, for it is far more profound than the best wisdom of humankind. God's strength and success is demonstrated in what we think is weakness and failure. You know"—Paul smirked—"however clever we think we are, it is all still silliness to God! Our knowledge is ever only partial.

"Finally, don't do what you know is wrong. Rather, whatever is true, whatever is honorable and just, whatever is pure and wholesome, whatever is commendable, think and do these things. Those who are apathetic—be active! Those of you with faint hearts—be encouraged! Be patient with everyone, for none of us is perfect. Help everyone you know who is in need, especially the poor, the lonely, and the powerless. Always converse with God and be thankful in everything. Partner with God, work hard, and work together with each other, for there is much to be done. And remember, the power of love overcomes all disputes. Peace be with you all."

An error message flashed simultaneously on to all the projection screens indicating that this unprecedented satellite connection was terminated. Nothing the technicians tried could retrieve the link. Liam and the entire conference audience were stunned into silence.

Chapter Nine

THE APOCALYPSE

A Modern Paraphrase from the Original Greek Text.

EXCERPTS FROM THE TRANSLATOR'S INTRODUCTION.

THE APOCALYPSE OF TIMOTHY is an interesting text recently discovered in the Vatican Archives. Sadly, parts of the manuscript are damaged and illegible; experts think that approximately 90 percent of the text is present. Although a vigorous search has been carried out for other copies in all the major international libraries of antiquity, no other version of the document has yet been found.

Concerning its authorship. The Greek vocabulary is of such a poor quality that most scholars regard this text as written by someone for whom Greek was definitely not his/her first language. Consequently, it cannot possibly be have written by the Timothy associated with Paul, the apostle to the Gentiles. It is possible that the author's real name actually was Timothy. But it is more likely that, by using the name of Paul's friend and missionary companion, the author was using this pseudonym to lend authority to the contents of the text. Furthermore, we cannot claim to have discovered a lost manuscript because no other ancient texts refer to the biblical Timothy as having written an Apocalypse.

Concerning the manuscript's date. There are no specific historical or political references made within the text, so it is difficult to date (or place the writing of) the manuscript from its context alone. However, the specific mention of a "wealthy Western church" may indicate a medieval origin, certainly after the separation of the Eastern and Western churches. Therefore the earliest date of writing is probably near the end of the eleventh century CE. That, however, is highly contentious and some scholars consider it a modern forgery. This is because the work does not appear to have been circulated within Christian communities. (Otherwise, we would have other historical evidence for the existence of this work in church records and letters.) Unless the author was a medieval maverick, the embedded theology within the text is more in keeping with a very late, possibly contemporary, date. A further reason for a recent date is the marked lack of reference to flamboyant Old Testament imagery and symbolism that is typical of this genre of literature. Certainly this would have occurred had the text been written in the Middle Ages. Some in the media think the Roman Catholic Church has suppressed this document for theological and, perhaps, political reasons. Most serious scholars think this conjecture is unlikely.

Given this manuscript's questionable provenance, what value does this text have for the Church today? We shall simply have to see how church congregations respond. A formal translation, however, may give more scholarly credence to the manuscript than is merited, given the poor quality Greek, its inconclusive dating, and the fact we do not have the original text in its entirety. Consequently a paraphrase, where the essential meaning of the text is preserved, is widely deemed more appropriate. I therefore present this modern paraphrase with the fervent hope that the spirit of the author's intention is faithfully presented.

THE APOCALYPSE OF TIMOTHY

Chapter 1

A revelation of Jesus Christ, given to him by God, in order to communicate wisdom to Christ's faithful followers in the Western churches. Christ made this revelation known to his faithful minister Timothy through God's angelic messenger called Malakai. Blessed are the ones who read, study, and respond to all that is written herein.

From Timothy to the Western church. Grace and peace to you from Jesus the Christ, who was, and is, and is to come; the first fruit of the bodily resurrection.

I, Timothy, was sitting in my study praying for inspiration as I was composing my message for Sunday. In front of me sat an open Bible, seven commentaries, and my preliminary sermon notes when I heard a loud knock at the door. I called out, "Come in."

The door opened and the room was ablaze with light as if the sun had entered. The light blinded me momentarily, leaving me disoriented and full of fear. Then I heard a familiar voice call out my name. Instinctively, I fell to my knees with my eyes tightly shut, for fear of becoming blind. I cried out, "Speak, Lord, for your servant is listening."

Then, being overwhelmed, I lay as one slain in the Spirit before the Son. The bright light faded. Then I heard a voice saying, "Relax and be at peace. And write down all that I will show you through my messenger Malakai.

He will speak my words to you, a message to be revealed to wealthy Western churches."

Being reassured, I opened one eye and glimpsed the source of the voice. I saw a lion with a large golden mane. A fine specimen of a creature that was much larger than I had expected. My pulse raced, yet the look in the lion's eyes reassured me. I knew that if the lion had wanted to end my life, it would have already happened. "Sit up," said the lion, "and meet Malakai, the messenger who will accompany you on your journey."

Malakai was about eight feet tall and wearing flowing white robes. The color of his skin was like nothing I had seen before. He was clean-shaven and had brown hair. His demeanor was casual, inviting. In my confused state the word *journey* surfaced to my consciousness. I returned my gaze to the king of beasts and blurted out in excitement, "Where to? Are you going to give me a glimpse of heaven?"

"No," said the lion, "Malakai is taking you for a tour of Hell!"

I was horrified. The last thing I wanted was to write down everything about this journey and become the laughing stock of my colleagues. Even worse, to have to admit that imaginative literalists were right after all. The Lion threw back his head and, shaking his magnificent mane, roared with laughter.

"I know what you're thinking," the lion said. "Relax, Timothy, I have chosen you for a purpose, to speak to the Church. I desire that they do something about what you see while there is still time. To partner with me and for what I value in new and creative ways."

With that, the lion vanished.

Malakai came and stood by me and said, "I will always be alongside you, Timothy, so do not be afraid on this brief visit to Hell. Remember this is a vision. We can see and hear the damned, yet they cannot see or hear us. Watch and absorb all that you experience. The Spirit will help you recall the details of this prophetic message."

Chapter 2

As Malakai finished saying his words, a whirlwind rushed through my study, tossing my papers and books throughout the room. Its intensity grew and, looking up, I could see daylight through the roof. The vortex of the tornado caught Malakai and me and took us away. Moments later all was quiet, and I saw a long corridor lined with closed secure doors. Both sides of the walls were covered with murals of bright yellow, orange, and red, making the corridor feel claustrophobic. The murals seemed alive—flames flared as you moved by and then stopped whenever you stood still. As we walked along the hallway, Malakai explained that there were three layers to hell.

Malakai opened a door and we went in. The room was in dim, predawn light. I could smell smoke from burning wood fires. As the light grew brighter I saw well-worn tents and dilapidated makeshift dwellings. Smoke rose from campfires being re-lit. Women and children milled about. Some were crying. All were dressed in rags and were dirty. Time accelerated for a moment and then I saw people with dejected faces and numbed from shock lining up to enter a larger tent. Inside were a few people, obviously medics of some sort, patching up the injured with sparse supplies. Everyone looked tired, clearly overwhelmed with the scale of this particular crisis. I saw bandaged children with missing limbs, some learning to walk with homemade crutches.

Malakai explained that this scene is just one of many camps. These are forgotten refugees with no identities and no place to call home. They have no voice and no advocates. No power to change their circumstances. They are hungry and afraid, lost souls with no hope.

"This is a *living* hell," he said. "You know that such places exist, but they are in some other land, and what is out of sight is also out of mind. Yet God is fully aware of such things."

I knew all too well that Malakai spoke the truth. Witnessing such a tragedy was very different from reading about it. Tears fell down my cheeks as I saw their plight.

"How do such things arise?" I asked.

Malakai then gave me a vision within a vision. He showed me the largest warehouse I had ever seen. There were millions of crates and specialized containers of various shapes and sizes. I also saw countless different kinds of vehicles; all were colored olive green. The immense scale and quantity was overwhelming.

Malakai spoke quietly, "These are all weapons and equipment of war, a gigantic array of ways to kill each other. God made you creative, but do you really think all this is the reason God made you?"

The vision ended, and Malakai and I looked on in silence over the refugee camp. After a while Malakai said, "Has history really shown that good can be achieved by means of violence? This tragedy is *not* what God intended. It is people who place other people in this layer of hell."

Then Malakai turned and looked at me. "The lion

says, 'Why does God need to make a Hell when you already have made one! Do you really think you should be entrusted with the stewardship of the New Earth, given your track record in tending the present one? That is why my rescue initiative was necessary, to save you from the systemic evils you have created. My reign has begun in order to permanently vanquish evil and all its effects in creation and in history. Is the Church going to work with me? Recall what I said to Peter, 'Look after my sheep!' Take care of the defenseless and vulnerable. Do not compound their problems by righteous apathy. Shame on those who sit comfortably at home aware of their plight and do nothing to help. Damned are those who cause them to doubt that their Father in heaven is a loving God and passionately committed to them.'"

I was stunned by Malakai's message from the Lord. He sensed my reaction and continued in a gentler way. "It is through you, the Church, that God wants to bless the world. When Jesus returns he expects to find you busy, not idle. Do you think that those in this living Hell are really doomed? Do you think that God will condemn those who have been forgotten, abused, and suffered at the hands of humans? Do you think that God's bountiful grace will not cover all such people, throughout both space and time? Does not the Scripture say, 'To anyone who is thirsty Christ will give the right to drink from the water of life without paying for it'?"[13]

CHAPTER 3

Malakai then took me to the next layer down in Hell and we walked along the corridor. The colors in the murals were more intense, and their animation more vibrant and alive. It was stifling. Even the hallway itself seemed hotter than the level above.

Malakai opened one of the doors and we went in. What I saw was utter chaos. There were people of all nations, many of them in smart work suits, scrambling and fighting over bits of paper. Some people sat on the floor exhausted, regaining strength before re-entering the fray. A piece of paper drifted my way and I caught it. It was money. All these people were fighting over money. I noticed that some people had organized themselves into small groups, and went over to listen to their conversation. They spoke as if they were from the financial sector. They were speaking of "moving money around," banking, interest rates, and profit and loss. The reality of the situation seemed farcical, a bizarre and sick game. For they could spend it on nothing, as there was nothing to purchase. Malakai explained, "In life, humankind *per se* did not matter to them. They had no purpose but to get richer and richer by whatever means they could. They lost their souls, and that is why this is their hell. They have lost all sense of what it means to be creatures made in God's image, and even now they do not want to acknowledge that fact. Money is their idol and they worship it. They are addicted to it, so now they have their hearts' desire. People put themselves in this layer of Hell; they still prefer darkness to light."

We left the room and the corridor seemed more oppressive than before. This experience was depressing and disorientating—nothing like what I expected.

The next room was different in that I was looking down on a vast array of private cubicles, each containing one person. Each individual was continually ranting, swearing, and shouting words of hatred. They each had what seemed like an indestructible stick that was being used to batter their surrounding walls, as if responding to the thuds on the walls from their invisible nearest neighbors.

"What is going on?" I asked Malakai.

"This is an isolation suite for those who worshipped and abused power," he said. "Even now, after personally meeting the living Christ, these people remain unremorseful and have hearts filled with hatred, only desiring aggression. They can't do violence to anyone now, however hard they try. Nor can they be empowered, as there is no one to victimize. For the moment, this experience is their chosen hell; they have their hearts' yearning..."

[Manuscript break]

"Are we going to the third level?" I asked.

"For the moment there are some mysteries neither you nor I know," Malakai said. "No one knows about the lowest level of Hell but God alone."

"But you must have some ideas about it," I said imploringly. Malakai closed his eyes and was silent for a while, as if meditating. Then he said carefully, "Some angels speculate that its entrance is the Door to Nowhere through which some will eventually choose to pass through. Others claim it is yet to be occupied. All I can say for certain is that it is very quiet in that level."

"Can't you say more?" I asked, "Don't you know how much this issue concerns us humans?"

Malakai grinned, without dismissing the seriousness of the issue. "All angels agree that God reserves the right to place those beings who remain totally self-absorbed, even after a time in the previous level, in this third layer of Hell. But many of us wonder if he has the will to actually do it. Not that God is weak-willed, far from it! God's gracious restraint is a sign of the strength of his will."

"But what do *you* think?" I asked.

Yet again, Malakai was silent. He then continued in a quieter tone. "My personal opinion, based on my understanding of God's character, is that it remains vacant as a testament to God's grace and the Son's supreme love gift. I know how much God values and respects the free will given to all responsible beings. Even so, our loving God is very patient and I suspect even the second layer of Hell is only temporary and then..."

[Manuscript break]

"...Door to Nowhere."

[Manuscript break]

"...we angels wait and wonder, as you do..."

[Manuscript break]

CHAPTER 4

Back in my study, as if we had never left, Malakai said, "Jesus says to you, 'Timothy, tell this message to my faithful ones in the Church. You are like a plant within a clay pot, which at first glance looks healthy, but is in fact rootbound. Your spiritual growth is stunted. You are not living up to your full potential, not experiencing the abundance of life that my Spirit so wants to give you. Some are self-righteously unaware of their plight. Others have life but are afraid to go deeper. Are you on a journey towards me or are you content to stay where you are? Some say longingly, 'There must be more than this!' To which Jesus says 'There is, believe me!'

"'Once your soil was healthy and full of energy. That goodness is now gone and your roots are choking for life. You can only live on water and sunlight for so long. You need fresh nutrients. What I long to do,' says Jesus, 'is to break the clay pot that is constraining your roots and to transplant you. I want to place you in a deeper and wider pot. It contains richer soil for your roots to spread and experience new vitality that my Spirit longs to give, and to lead you into more authentic worship. But you are disinterested and are not cooperating with me. Some of you have idols that take my place, such as wealth, rule-keeping, self-image, church politics, programs, traditions, and buildings. And yes, even the Scriptures, and your intellect! Many are for the best of intentions but are missing the essential point.

"'What I want for you is to know *me*, the risen Christ, to relate with me, both as individuals and as a community, so that you will make a real difference in the world. Through you I want to bless the world and all creation. Many of you are living off a past legacy. For some, one that is centuries old. You once had a compassionate heart and were outward-looking, but now you are divided and you squabble. Competitive, not cooperative; suspicious, not trusting.

"'Work together, work with any who share my values of justice, fairness, and mercy. Do not misunderstand me. I am not seeking a utopia—an earthly paradise made by human hands. I am not interested in a theocracy, a political solution. I never was. But all that is truly good will be transformed into the new Earth when my reign comes in its fullness.'"

Chapter 5

"These words are true and can be trusted," Malakai said. "The Lord God, who gives his Spirit to his prophets and to the Church, has given you a glimpse of what needs to be done. Jesus says 'I am coming again. Happy are those who hear and respond to these prophetic words written in this book.'"

I, Timothy, saw and heard all these things. Come Lord Jesus and find your children working for your Kingdom.

Grace and peace of our Savior Jesus Christ be with you all.

FOR FURTHER THOUGHT
Suggested Bible Readings and Discussion Questions

The following suggested Bible readings mirror the themes and stories within this book. They can be used together with the discussion questions to consider more deeply how each chapter applies to you. While you can do this on your own or in a group context, I recommend the latter. Hearing others' perspectives has the potential to be mutually beneficial. The questions are not meant to be fixed or exhaustive, simply a starting point to stimulate meaningful discussion. Enjoy!

CHAPTER 1: THE DAWN

READ GENESIS 2:4b–3:24

Compare and contrast the Genesis account of life in the garden and the Fall of humankind with that described in *The Dawn*.

1. What were your thoughts and feelings as you read the story? What aspects did you enjoy? What features surprised you? Were there elements you found puzzling? Did you find yourself reacting in any intense way? If so, reflect on why you responded as you did. Did you find anything refreshing or helpful?
2. List the various ways Terrene's dawn of heightened self-consciousness is expressed within the story. How do they relate to the Christian view that humankind is created in the image of God (Genesis 1:26-7)? How are you aware of your own God-given identity?
3. The location where God resides was portrayed as a

kingly court in the story (see also Genesis 1:26, 3:22). How do you imagine "heaven"—or God's present domain? Is it an exciting hive of activity, or more like one power figure on a large throne, or something else? Do you regard God as being very distant from human affairs, or closely involved? What do these stories tell us? Is that surprising? If so, why?

4. The Maker is intimately concerned with Terrene and Zoë, and befriends them at their moment of need. Is that your expectation and experience of God? How so?

5. A common perception is that the "Fall" of humankind (Genesis 3) was a fall *downward* from a state of perfection. Some see the Fall as falling *upward*, with the maturation of humankind's consciousness and the development of moral responsibility. Others regard the Fall as a falling *outward*, out of relationship with our Maker, each other, and the created order. What thoughts or reactions do you have to these three views? To which are you most drawn, and why? In Genesis 1:31 God declares everything in creation as "very good." How do you connect that acclamation with these three views on the Fall?

6. Not only does the Maker inform Terrene and Zoë of their identity, but also their responsibilities. What does the Maker say these are (see also Genesis 1:26-30)? Are you participating in the responsibilities that God has given humankind? If so, in what ways?

7. Authentic love and free will are powerful realities, yet both have an element of mystery about them. Whatever you have thought about these topics before, how—if anything—does this story challenge, enhance, or alter your understanding of them?

Chapter 2: The Amish Farmer Who Hated L.A.

Read Jonah 1:1–17; 2:10–4:11 and Jeremiah 18:1–11

Compare and contrast what you imagine the lifestyles of Bill and Mervin to be. How do the differences form the backdrop to the story? With whom do you most identify?

1. In what ways do Mervin's attitudes mirror those of Jonah?
2. Identify what you found to be the humorous, ironic, or perhaps even absurd elements of both stories.
3. In Jonah's context, the underlying assumption is that no Jew would want God to show mercy to one of their traditional enemies, the Assyrian Empire (Nineveh). In this story, God says to Mervin: "Know that my love crosses boundaries that you do not think possible or appropriate." Who do you consider as unsuitable—or somehow less likely to be—recipients of God's love and mercy? When you think of God, is your image like that of Jonah's who knew of God's gracious heart but did not like it (4:2)?
4. Taking Jonah as post-exilic literature, it was written at a time when Jews in the restored homeland were very conservative and thought that to please God they should remain separate from their neighboring cultures. The story of Jonah challenges that attitude and thereby was a critique of their narrow, exclusive view of God. In the story, God says to Mervin: "Know there will be more people in my Kingdom than you think!" How does this message challenge us today?
5. Jonah is a kind of "anti-hero"; a reluctant follower of God with firm, preconceived ideas about what God should and should not do. And yet was a remarkably

successful prophet. Upon hearing the warning, Nineveh repented! How do we limit God by our preconceived ideas of what God is like or our judgment on how God should act?
6. God says to Jonah (twice, Jonah 4:4, 9): "Is it right for you to be angry?" Are you angry at God for any reason? Are you, like Mervin and Jonah, running away from God, or from what you know is right?
7. What do you think God might be trying to say to you through this story today?

Chapter 3: The God-Man Project

Read John 1:1-18 and Philippians 2:5-11

Wouldn't it be literally awesome to be a fly-on-the-wall at the heavenly court? We have so many questions we would like to ask God face-to-face! This imaginary story gives a brief glimpse of what it might be like to witness a heavenly committee meeting. These descriptions of the divine realm are, of course, based on pure fantasy—so don't try to see inference or meaning where there is none!

1. If Raphael were to give a speech on the emotional and spiritual mood of your country today, what would be said? If Jophiel were to report on the social and political scene in your region today, what would he say?
2. The story attempts to describe God's thought processes and rationale for history. Does that narrative resonate with what you imagine? If so, in what ways? If not, how would you express it?
3. Are there elements of the Maker's speech that you find troubling or disturbing? If so, what is about them that is disconcerting to you?

4. Do you think that God *really* understands you and the vulnerability of the human experience? Does the incarnation—God becoming human in the form of his son, Jesus— influence your response? Explain your reasoning.
5. The story portrays God as being both sovereign and freely choosing to be "self-limiting." What is your reaction to this idea? What do you suppose has shaped your viewpoint? Does this perspective render God as "too weak" or, ironically, "even stronger" in your mind? Explore this notion.
6. War correspondents are sometimes described by their fellow journalists as "embedded with the troops." Do you regard the earthly Jesus as being truly "embedded with humanity," as one of us? If so, how? If not, why?
7. What did you like about this story? What did you not like? Reflect on why you think/feel that way.
8. How does this story affect your view of God? Of Jesus?

CHAPTER 4: THE FIRST DAY

Read Matthew 4:1–11 and/or Luke 4:1–13

A temptation is not a *real* temptation unless we are genuinely vulnerable to its charm. Do you think Jesus was really tempted? Why do you think that way?

1. Carlos Rodriguez's temptations were the triplet of money, sex, and power. What temptations do you face at work, or in your daily routine? In your home life? In your leisure activities? Be honest with yourself.
2. What were the temptations that Jesus faced? Why do you think Matthew's and Luke's accounts of the life of Jesus state that he was particularly vulnerable to those

temptations rather than others? How might the Gospel writers be relating those specific temptations to point out Jesus' identity?
3. When you experience temptation, how do you react? What strategies do you employ to resist them? What approach do the Gospel writers say that Jesus took? How is your approach similar or different? Do you find his tactics helpful?
4. Temptations often arise when we are alone, weak, and vulnerable, as was the case for Jesus in the Gospel accounts. Recall that Jesus was just about to start his ministry and had yet to form his band of disciples. How can being connected to others within a community help you in resisting temptation? Think of practical, realistic strategies how this might be helpful and effective for you. How might you implement them?
5. How could you be a part of the solution for someone else's encounters with temptation?

CHAPTER 5: THE SERMON

READ LUKE 10:25–37, MARK 12:28–34, AND ISAIAH 55:1–11

The story begins in the setting of a church service. For those who attend a church, how does this portrayal of Christian worship make you feel? Why is that? What is your vision of an "ideal" church service? How does it compare with George's view?

1. When you think of the parables of Jesus, how do you regard them? Quaint? Edgy? As a cultural or spiritual critique? What are the advantages and disadvantages in using parables—or stories—to get a point across?
2. Jesus addressed the parable to an expert in Mosaic Law.

How does that fact feature in the parable? What parallels can you see in *The Sermon*?

3. Compare Steve's journey with that of the man's in Luke 10:30-35. What surprises you in the story and why does it?

4. Why is it, do you think, that when we are in a position to help we often fail to act? The politician in the story failed to give assistance because of fear (followed by forgetfulness). Have you ever been in a situation where the thought of risk to your personal safety stopped you from intervening? If so, relate the incident. With hindsight, would you have done anything differently? Explain.

5. The TV Evangelist did not demonstrate compassion because he was in a hurry and did not want to be inconvenienced. We live in a fast-paced society where everybody is busy. What strategies could you employ to create time for those in real need?

6. The Muslim biker, a visiting tourist, does what Steve's fellow citizens fail to do. He demonstrates compassion at some personal expense. In what ways is the hero in the story similar to the Samaritan in Jesus' parable?

7. Why do we find "loving our neighbors as ourselves" so hard (Luke 10:27)? Who is *your* neighbor?

8. Despite Darryl's negative reaction from his church, Congressman Watson was intrigued enough to want to know more (see Isaiah 55:11). What does the Bible say about the reaction to Jesus' parable (see also Mark 12:28-34)? What is your reaction?

CHAPTER 6: THE JOURNEY

READ ACTS 3: 1–10 AND JOHN 20:19–31

What do you think of miracles and those who make miraculous claims? Why is that? Can you relate to Martin Wright's perspective?

1. If you have met people like Martin, how do you react? Compare that to Kevin's reaction.
2. Would you describe yourself as a skeptic? How do you think Jesus responds to skeptics?
3. Have you, like Kevin, ever been "affronted with a genuine miracle that defies rational explanation"? If so, when? And how did you react?
4. When you hear of stories in the Old Testament, like that mentioned in Joshua (see Joshua 10:12-14) or those associated with, say, Elijah, do you tend to regard them as *literal* or *literary* history? Why is that? Can you respect God-honoring alternative understandings—like the one Kevin relates concerning Joshua?
5. Reflection: Is there only "one" way to read and interpret the Bible? How do you think of—and behave towards—other Christians who do not agree with your own perspective?
6. What is your reaction to the Gospel accounts of Jesus walking on water and calming the storm (Mark 4:35-41; 6:45-51)?
7. We are familiar with the magical worlds of *Lord of the Rings* and the *Harry Potter* saga. Do you find it helpful, as C. S. Lewis did, to regard the Gospel miracles as "myths that actually happened"? Why or why not?
8. Is your worldview one that is dominated by the use of reason (i.e. a scientific worldview or modernism)?[14] How do you respond to postmodern ideas?[15] Such ideas are present in our Western culture—and there is no going back.

How does this reality impact upon your faith journey?
9. How much of your understanding about God has been unquestioningly embraced or uncritically absorbed from your upbringing and/or faith community? How have you wrestled with complex theological issues, using the tools of Scripture, reason, tradition, and experience, to deepen and expand your understanding of God and his purposes?

Chapter 7: The Nightmare

Read Acts 10:1–11:18

Luke, the author of Acts, deemed this incident to be so important that he tells the story twice. Some would say this encounter was as much a "conversion" of Peter as of Cornelius.

1. Identify the parallels between the story of Peter and Cornelius and that of Lloyd and Perwira. What aspects of Luke's story come to life for you?
2. Are their elements to Lloyd's nightmare that you find troubling? If so, what are they and why are they so disconcerting? Why was Peter troubled by his vision within a first-century Jewish context?
3.. How Christians relate to people of other faiths and traditions in a multicultural setting is relevant throughout the world, especially in urban centers. Perhaps surprisingly, there are strong similarities to the city-states of the first-century Greco-Roman world—but for different historical reasons. Jesus, Peter, and Paul all came into contact with "God-fearers" (or "those who honored God"). In certain cases, Jesus praised their faith, much to the chagrin of fellow Jews.[16] What do you think Jesus might say in today's multicultural context?

4. As followers of Jesus, we are sent into the world to pass on the Good News. How does this story affect your views as to how that might be done?
5. Whatever we do in that regard, both stories make it clear that the Holy Spirit will have already gone before us. How do you respond to that idea? How do you recognize the Spirit at work in others?
6. If you were in Lloyd's shoes, what would you have done in Perwira's home? What would you advise Lloyd to say and do upon his return to his church in the US?
7. What have you learned about God's Spirit in this story?
8. What have you learned about *God's* mission?

Chapter 8: The Audience

Read from this selection: 1 Corinthians 12:4–13:13; Galatians 3:28, 5:22–23; 1 Corinthians 1: 18–25; Romans 8:35–39; and Philippians 4:4–9

Besides Jesus—and with no disrespect to Peter—Paul is arguably the most influential person in church history. Not simply because he founded a string of Christian communities throughout the Roman Empire, but because many of Paul's writings are preserved for us, providing a unique window to his life and work. Paul's letters were addressed to churches, so the contents of *The Audience* are appropriately addressed to churches today.

1. What is your reaction to the story? How much of that reflects your personal bias? What alternative message do you think Paul might say today—and why? Paul was skilled in literary rhetoric. After reading his analogy of the body (1 Corinthians 12:12-31) and this story's one of a computer, what other contemporary metaphors or images might you use to make Paul's point(s) in a fresh way?

2. What is your church community actively doing to enhance Christian unity? How is that going?
3. In this story, baptism is highlighted as a unifying symbol for Christians. Do you see it this way today? If not, what alternative(s) do you suggest? Give reasons.
4. In I Corinthians 13, Paul emphasizes love as key. Does this story's description of love help you actualize its profound meaning? How would you express it? Have you ever experienced such love, or even a glimmer of it? Where? How can you become a better agent of such radical love in today's world?
5. If Christian leaders publically admitted their mistakes or misunderstandings, how would that affect you? Why?
6. Are you, like Paul, "free from the anxiety of the finality of death"? What is your vision of the cosmic future? Restoration? Gloom? Why is that? What are the grounds of Paul's confidence? What do you think of his reason(s)?
7. Are you, overall, inspired and encouraged by what Paul has to say in this story? What aspects resonated with you most? What did you find most challenging? Is there anything that gives you hope or peace of mind?

CHAPTER 9: THE APOCALYPSE

READ REVELATION 20:11–21:11, 21:22–22:7 AND MATTHEW 25:31–46.

The images of John the Seer, though very strange to us, build on similar apocalyptic visions of earlier Jewish prophets, like Daniel and Zephaniah. Rather than becoming bogged in the details, try to envision the broader canvas. It is one where all hopes are fulfilled, all injustices are addressed, and where God's reign comes in its fullness, bringing *shalom*—peace with God, our neighbor, and with creation.

1. Try to identify the images and metaphors alluded to in Chapter 1 of Timothy's apocalypse. What added insight, if any, does that give you?[17]
2. In the story, the first layer of hell is described as "a *living* hell." Alas, for far too many on our planet that is the reality. Malakai says: "This tragedy is *not* what God intended. It is people who place other people in this layer of hell." What do you think of this claim? Discuss your reasoning.
3. Malakai's commentary on the second layer of hell is: "People put *themselves* in this layer of Hell." The implication is that God continues to honor our free will, but there are, nevertheless, consequences to our choices and actions. If this is the case, do you think that God is being fair or acting justly? Why is that? How do you try to balance God's justice and mercy?[18]
4. In the story, the details of the third layer of hell remain a mystery. Do you think that this is a copout? Why is that? If you think the third layer is more definitively knowable, then suggest an alternative ending. On what grounds do you base your description of the third layer of hell?
5. Back in Timothy's study, Malakai relates a metaphor of a plant growing in a pot. How would you describe your soil and the health of the plant that corresponds to your life?
6. Prophetic visions are, among other things, meant to exhort, rebuke, cajole, as well as inspire hope and empower transformational change. What is your reaction to the story?
7. Where do you go from here?

Endnotes

[1] *Midrash* is a form of storytelling in Rabbinic literature that adds a clarifying commentary to a scriptural text, often exploring things left unsaid by the text.

[2] See Proverbs 16:33

[3] See Joshua 10:12-14.

[4] See Mark 6:45-51

[5] See Mark 4:35-41

[6] See Acts 10:34-35.

[7] See Ephesians 5:22.

[8] See Galatians 3:28.

[9] See Galatians 2:11-14.

[10] 1 Corinthians 13:13.

[11] D. J. Hall, *The Cross in Our Context* (Minneapolis: Fortress Press, 2003), 224.

[12] D. J. Hall, *The Cross in Our Context* (Minneapolis: Fortress Press, 2003), 214.

[13] See Revelation 21:6; 22:17, and Isaiah 55:1.

[14] Modernism was shaped by the Enlightenment, with its desire for greater personal freedom from established authorities, such as monarchs, Church, tradition, and revelation (i.e. religious texts). This quest led to an emphasis on the rational, autonomous individual with public truth being determined by the use of reason and the scientific method, rather than by religious dogma or subjective faith. Modernism fueled a spirit of cultural optimism empowered by consumer capitalism and technological advances which resulted in a progressive Western society, along with the modern notions of human rights, personal freedoms, democracy, nation-state, and citizenship.

[15] Post-modernism is a critical and reactive movement *after* or *beyond* modernism. Rather than modernism's emphasis on classification and objectivity, post-modernism celebrates difference (pluralism) and

context (relativism), resulting in a worldview with no external absolutes for making choices. Consequently there is no unique overarching, or transcendent, storyline to history from which one has a basis to construct social order or guide individuals.

[16] For example, see Matt 8:5-13.

[17] The cryptic images in Revelation are also meant to enhance, not detract from, its message.

[18] There are, I suggest, two extremes in addressing the topic of hell, both of which are, alas, too common. One is an overemphasis of "hell" and "end times" speculation, and therefore fostering a culture of judgment, fear, and insecurity. The other denies the reality of hell or a final accountability before God, thereby belittling God's justice by having an over-emphasis on God's mercy. I do not advocate either extreme; but if we are to err on one side, then I suggest it should be on that of God's mercy. Matthew 19:30-20:16 and Luke 13:22-30 suggest there will be surprises on that "last day"!

CONNECT WITH TIM:
email—tim.j.reddish@gmail.com
website—asamatteroffaith.com